ABOUT THE AUTHOR

Subhadra Sen Gupta has written over forty books for children because she thinks children are the best readers in the world. In 2014 she won the Bal Sahitya Puraskar for her children's books. She loves telling stories woven around history; plotting mysteries and adventures; dreaming up ghostly tales and scripting comic books. So if you want to start a conversation with her, write to her at subhadrasg@gmail.com.

PAINTERS POTTERS COOKS AND KINGS

SUBHADRA SEN GUPTA

Illustrations
Tapas Guha

SCHOLASTIC
New York Toronto London Auckland
Sydney New Delhi Hong Kong

For my sister Sushmita,
Generous provider of gourmet meals,
Good books and awful jokes. With love.

Published by Scholastic India Pvt. Ltd.
A subsidiary of Scholastic Inc., New York, 10012 (USA).
Publishers since 1920, with international operations in Canada, Australia, New Zealand, the United Kingdom, India, and Hong Kong.

For information regarding permission, write to:
Scholastic India Pvt. Ltd.
A-27, Ground Floor, Bharti Sigma Centre
Infocity-1, Sector 34, Gurgaon-122001 (India)

ISBN-13: 978-93-5275-532-5

This Reprint Edition April,2024

Printed at Ram Printograph Delhi

CONTENTS

THE CALL OF THE VIHARA

6

Prince Siddhartha was born in the kingdom of K-a-p-i-l-a…er…v-a-s-t-u …’ Parvati’s voice was beginning to fade. ‘Uff! This is hard to read!’

Eyes focussed, frowning away, she bent over the pages of the manuscript as she ran her forefinger along the line of Pali text. ‘… to King Shuddho…ummm…dhana and Queen Maha…maya.’ She stopped to take a breath and looked up, her eyes wide. ‘How am I doing?’

‘Really well!’ the Buddhist monk, Bhikkhu Aditya, smiled. ‘I thought you’d get stuck on “Shuddhodhana”. That’s a long word.’

The three children, Parvati, Laxman and Nakul, were reading pages from a palm leaf manuscript in the study hall of the vihara, the Buddhist monastery where Aditya lived. He sat cross-legged before them in his saffron robes, his shaved head bent over a book on the life of the Buddha, teaching them to read. And occasionally when the children stumbled badly, he would patiently correct them.

Parvati's older brother, Laxman, held out another leaf of the book and asked, 'What's this word?'

Aditya peered at the page. 'Oh! This is another tough one—Dhammachakra pravartana.'

Their puzzled faces made Aditya grin. Somehow he always found their stumbling efforts at reading very funny.

'It means turning the wheel of Dhamma.'

'What wheel?' Laxman's friend Nakul frowned.

'After gaining enlightenment at Bodh Gaya, the Buddha gave his first sermon on Dhamma at a place called Sarnath.'

'Dhamma?'

'Our religion that is based on the teachings of the Buddha is called Dhamma. We also call him the Sakyamuni because he belonged to the tribe of the Sakya. With the sermon at Sarnath, he is said to have got the wheel of Dhamma turning.' Looking at their perplexed faces, Aditya began to laugh. 'I think this book is a bit too difficult for you. Tomorrow we'll go back to some simple Jataka tales.'

'Yes please,' Parvati nodded her curly head. 'I like reading stories; they are much more interesting than wheels turning.'

‘Now you three go home,’ Aditya stood up. ‘I have work to do.’

‘Oh good! My eyes are beginning to ache and I’m also feeling hungry!’ Parvati stood up.

‘There are bananas in that bowl on the shelf,’ Aditya pointed, and then began gathering up the palm leaf pages and tying them together. Then he placed the pages between two strips of wood, tied them again, wrapped them up in a cloth bundle and stacked them on a shelf in the vihara library. The manuscripts were both precious and fragile and Aditya was very careful with them.

The three children wandered out of the monastery munching on the bananas. Laxman and Parvati were the children of a potter and Nakul’s father was a weaver. Usually children of craftspeople were not taught to read and write, but these kids were very lucky. They lived near the vihara where Aditya taught them in the afternoons after his work was done.

They walked down the narrow lanes of the city of Pataliputra, the capital of the kingdom of Magadha. As they crossed the main street, the children had to dodge men riding horses and driving bullock carts, though most of the people walked. It was summer and the sun was high and people hurried past, carrying woven reed umbrellas, and after the cool, shady halls of the vihara, the hot and dusty streets made them sweat.

‘Dhammachakra pravartana … uff, what a huge word!’ Parvati muttered. ‘It takes forever just to say it.’

'How do you do that?' Nakul frowned at her.

'Do what?' Parvati turned to stare at Nakul.

'Remember things. You never forget a poem you hear or a word you read.'

'Who knows!' she shrugged, busy munching. 'I just can.'

'Yesterday Amma was asking what we do at the vihara,' Nakul said. 'I told her we are helping Aditya in the garden.'

Laxman nodded. 'Right! This is our secret. My parents don't want me to study either, because they think it's a waste of time. Amma wants me to work instead, making pots and helping Baba sell them.'

'Also our parents know that the rich people, the Brahmins and Kshatriyas, don't like it. Remember how the servants of a nobleman beat up that poor washerman because he learnt to write the numbers? All he wanted to do was keep a count of the clothes he was washing. What was wrong with that?'

'Ballabh, that fat priest at the temple,' Parvati added, 'says that the holy books would become dirty if we shudras touched them.' There was a touch of sadness in her eyes. 'It seems we belong to an unclean caste.'

Nakul shook his head angrily. 'Then how is it that the books at the vihara are just fine? And we touch them every day!'

'Lucky our king became a follower of the Buddha,' Laxman said as they exchanged smiles, 'and Aditya became a monk.'

It was fun to do something they were not supposed to do. They all knew the story of how their king His

Majesty Ashoka Vardhan of the Maurya dynasty had begun to follow the teachings of the Sakyamuni. After winning the battle at Kalinga, he saw all the dead and injured soldiers and decided that he would never fight a war again. He became a follower of Buddhism. Then he began to set up monasteries called viharas and soon the people discovered that the Buddhist monks who lived in the viharas were kind and generous people who led very simple lives. They went begging every morning for food and ate what they were given. They stitched old clothes and dyed them saffron to make robes for themselves. They all worked in the vihara, cooking, cleaning, stitching and gardening.

That was how they met Aditya. He came every morning to their door to beg, and Parvati would run to put a handful of rice and some vegetables into his begging bowl. The young monk would stand silently at their door wearing his patched robes and smile at her as she came skipping out. Then, gradually, they began to talk, and he invited them to the vihara where they found him reading. He happily agreed to teach them.

***

The next morning Laxman's father sat up in bed, coughing. He then gasped, 'I have to deliver the pottery today.'

Laxman's mother looked up from stirring a pot of dal and shook her head. 'No you won't! Your cough is so bad, and you hardly slept last night. Let the children take them today.'

'That would be good,' he sighed with relief and then turned to Laxman. 'You have to take the kitchen things to the pottery shop in the market. And see those earthen lamps? On your way back, deliver them at the temple, but make sure Ballabh pays you first. He always makes excuses. Tell him—no money, no lamps.'

'I know what he'll say,' Laxman grinned. 'That if we give them for free, Lord Shiva and Devi Durga will bless us.'

His father smiled. 'And then he'll ask you to pay for ghee for the lamps ...'

'Which his wife will use in her cooking,' their mother said shortly. 'How else do you think he's got so fat? He can hardly move!'

Laxman and Parvati loaded the bullock cart with the pottery—bowls, plates, glasses and cooking pans—and headed to the market. It was past noon when they got to the temple.

Ballabh came out, looking his usual fat sweaty self, wearing a white antariya tied like a dhoti. His head was shaved except for a pigtail. He wore the Brahmin thread across his bare chest and wooden slippers. There were gold rings in his ears, thick bangles on his wrist and he had drawn three lines across his forehead with sandalwood. He was panting and looked very irritated. 'You are late! I need the lamps for the puja now!'

'Baba said the lamps are for twenty four panas,' Laxman stood before the cart, firmly blocking his way, 'and he said I have to take the money from you first.'

'What?' Ballabh's wife Vedavati had followed him out and glared at Laxman. 'Do you know who you are speaking to? How dare you insult a Brahmin priest!'

Vedavati wore a bright red antariya pleated at her waist and a white uttariya was wrapped over her body. As always, she was jangling with jewellery. The people in the locality said that she wore more jewellery than the goddess Durga herself.

'You want the gods to curse you?' Ballabh asked.

'Baba is not well,' Parvati explained. 'We need the money.'

'Fine! I'll do a puja for him.'

'He needs medicine,' Laxman said, 'not gangajal and tulsi leaves.'

Ballabh took a look at their determined faces and said, 'Fine, fine …' He opened the cloth bag that was tied to his waist and took out a few copper coins. Then Laxman had to stand there with his palms held out as he carefully dropped the coins from above, making sure he did not touch Laxman's hand.

Laxman counted the coins very carefully. 'Four panas more,' he said.

'Oh *really*!' With a sharp glare Ballabh dropped four more copper coins into his hand. 'Next time I'll get another potter.'

'You do that,' Laxman nodded, knowing very well that all the other potters in their lane refused to sell to Ballabh.

As the children began to unload the lamps at the temple door, Vedavati suddenly screamed, 'Don't touch the door, you stupid girl! Or I'll have to wash it with ganga jal.' Parvati quietly moved the lamps back.

As they headed home, Parvati asked grimly, 'I can touch the puja lamps made by my potter father but why can't I touch the temple door?'

'Nakul's father weaves the cloth the goddess wears but he can't enter the temple to do puja,' Laxman added. 'At the vihara we can go everywhere.'

'Who made these absurd rules?' Nakul wondered.

'The Brahmins, who else?'

'I wonder what Ballabh will do if he finds out I can read!' Parvati grinned. 'Not just a shudra, but a girl!'

'A disobedient shudra girl? Oh, the world will come to an end!'

***

A few days later when they entered the vihara, they were surprised to find the courtyard teeming with people. Usually it was quiet and deserted in the afternoons but now well-dressed men and women were getting out of chariots and palanquins and heading for the prayer hall called the chaitya. There was an air of celebration, with flower garlands wrapped around pillars and an arch of flowers and leaves over the gate. Monks were hurrying about, carrying platters and bowls, and they could hear the chanting of mantras and smell incense in the air.

'What's up?' Nakul looked around in wonder.

Just then Aditya came hurrying out. 'Oh, children, I forgot to tell you, today we have a special ceremony at the vihara and I have to help in the chaitya. We'll read again tomorrow.'

'What's happening?'

'It is a wonderful day! Twenty young men are joining the vihara as novice monks. They will be initiated into the sangha by our senior monks.'

'What's a sangha?'

'Our brotherhood of monks is called the sangha.'

'What about the nuns?' Parvati frowned at him.

'I stand corrected, Parvati!' Aditya grinned at her disapproving face. 'Of course, the sisterhood too is a part of the sangha.'

'Can we watch?'

'Of course! Go into the chaitya and sit at the back. The families of the novice monks will be sitting in front.'

They entered the chaitya and took their place, watching the busy scene. It was a rectangular hall with a high altar at one end. The walls were painted with pretty designs of flowers and leaves, and the doorway, windows and pillars had been decorated with flower garlands. On the altar there was a large round stone on which the feet of the Buddha had been carved, and it was covered with flower petals. There were bowls of incense everywhere, with the smoke filling the air with perfume, and tall lamps with many golden flames stood at the corners.

A row of monks clad in saffron robes sat beside the altar, chanting prayers, as the guests they had seen milling around outside now began to come in and sit down in front. They were all wearing finely woven antariyas and uttariyas, and jewellery that fascinated Parvati. She spotted rings, earrings, necklaces, bangles and bracelets on the upper arms, anklets and even hair pins of gold set with shiny jewels! The women had elaborate hairdos, and Parvati studied one woman going past who had her hair done in a long plait that was wrapped around in a gold string with small bells.

She was sitting next to an old woman who was turning a string of prayer beads in her fingers. She asked, 'Amma, who are these people?'

'See those young men with shaved heads and saffron robes sitting in front? They are becoming novice monks today. These are their families.'

'The novices all come from rich families, do they?'

'Some of them do. See that man who has just come in?' They turned to see a tall man stride in. 'That's General Shilaka who fought at Kalinga. Now he is a trusted adviser to the king and his son is a novice.' She gave a small happy sigh. 'But my grandson is also becoming a bhikkhu today and his father is a trader. Everyone is welcome in the world of the Sakyamuni.'

They watched Shilaka march grimly to the front and sit down. He had a thick moustache curling across a broad face and large eyes under bushy eyebrows. His broad shoulders and muscular arms were that of a warrior. Nakul noticed that he did not bow to the senior monks sitting in front like the other people were doing, and he did not smile. He looked around impatiently as if he did not like what he saw and was bored with the ceremony.

Then the initiation ceremony began. It was a simple affair, very different from the long and expensive pujas at Ballabh's temple. Each novice monk went up to the row of senior monks, kneeled before them, touched his forehead to the ground in greeting and then said, *Buddham saranam* (I take refuge in the Buddha), *Dhammam saranam* (I take refuge in Dhamma), *Sangham saranam* (I take refuge in the sangha).

The senior monks blessed them by raising their hands and then welcomed them by saying, 'Ehi bhikkhu!' which meant 'Come forth, O monk!'

'Is it over?' Nakul asked in surprise. 'It was done so quietly and peacefully!'

'Ehi Parvati! Ehi Nakul!' Laxman had learnt a new word. 'Let's go home. It's getting dark.'

Coming out of the chaitya, they noticed that the main gate was crowded with people, horses, chariots and palanquins, and so decided to take a short cut. They knew the layout of the vihara well and walked through the inner quadrangle, a square open space around which were the cells of the monks.

These tiny rooms just held a palette on the floor for the monks to sleep on, a small cushion and a wooden board on which they could lean when they sat for long hours, meditating. The monks owned very little except a couple of robes, a begging bowl, a pair of chappals, a hand fan and prayer beads. Parvati often thought even the poorest people in their lane had more possessions.

At the end of the quadrangle was the room of the head of the vihara, Prior Bhadraka, and as they were going past, they heard raised voices that made them stop in surprise. They knew that people did not argue loudly in the vihara and the monks always spoke softly.

'Your son chose this path, sir,' Bhadraka was saying calmly. 'It was his choice, and he is not a child.'

'What choice?' a loud, angry voice shouted. 'The boy's always been a fool, and you monks have influenced him. He never talked about joining the sangha until that bhikkhu Aditya became his friend. That smooth-talking monk convinced him!'

They peered in through a window and saw General Shilaka standing before Prior Bhadraka, hands on his hips, his face red, pointing an angry forefinger at Bhadraka. 'He is my son and he should be a warrior like me. Not a bald, bell-ringing, prayer-chanting bhikkhu.'

Bhadraka took a deep breath and said gently, 'Sir, if at any time your son feels he has made a mistake, he is free to leave the sangha. Our great teacher Gautama Buddha, the Sakyamuni, said you stay a monk only if you want that life.'

'He will leave. I'll make sure of that!' snapped Shilaka and then turned and marched out of the room.

***

As they wandered home, Nakul asked, puzzled, 'I thought becoming a monk was an honour. All the families looked so happy. Why was he so angry?'

'We must ask Aditya,' Parvati said. 'It seems Shilaka is angry with him too.'

As they turned into their lane, they heard the sound of bells and conches. The evening arati had started at the temple and they could hear Ballabh's voice loudly chanting the mantras.

Laxman peered inside and said, 'Oh, there aren't many people here!'

'Naturally! Everyone in the lane was at the vihara,' Parvati said.

'We got leaf plates of food after the ceremony when all Ballabh gives is one sugar batasha and a slice of soggy banana,' Nakul said.

'Ballabh was furious when all the rich merchants in our lane started visiting the vihara. No more expensive pujas!' Parvati remarked.

***

Next morning Laxman headed to the home of the vaid, the Ayurvedic physician, to get his father's cough medicine. Vaidji was an old man with a long white beard, his hair tied in a knot on top of his head, and wearing a thick cotton antariya. He sat at the verandah of his tiny brick and thatch house, grinding herbs and spices in a small stone mortar and pestle. Behind the house was a large garden where he grew the herbs that he used in his medicines.

Vaidji, who was short-sighted, looked up, recognised Laxman, smiled and asked, 'How's your father?'

'His cough is much better, Vaidji.'

'Good, good ... He needs one more week of the medicine and he'll be fine. Meanwhile, make sure he stays in bed.'

'Parvati and I have been delivering the pots so he can rest.'

The old man put a brown powder into seven small leaf packets. 'One packet every day of this bhasma churan is all he needs, and make him drink milk.'

'He says the powder is very bitter. What's it made of, Vaidji?'

'Heh ... heh ... the more bitter, the better! It's got dried ginger root, turmeric and my special chyavanprush.' He tied the packets with string and gave them to Laxman. 'That will be two panas.'

***

The vaid's home was next to the local market and Laxman had some shopping to do. He bought vegetables —spinach, cucumber, pumpkin, bitter gourd and some chana dal for their mother to cook for lunch. Right next to the vegetable shop was a lane in which there was a row of big mansions where some noblemen and rich traders lived. Laxman had been to many of the back gates of these houses to deliver pottery. He spotted Ballabh hurrying down the lane, panting, and wiping the sweat off his face with the end of his antariya.

'Fat Ballabh walking! Now that's quite a sight,' he thought. 'He never walks if he can help it.'

Feeling curious, he followed the priest into the lane and saw him stop at the second house on the left. It had a high gate with a guard holding a spear standing before it. Ballabh muttered something to the guard and was allowed inside.

'It looks like he's found himself a rich client!' Laxman grinned to himself.

For the next few days, Laxman and Parvati did not have time for lessons. As their father was still in bed, they had to work. Early one morning they walked to the banks of the Ganga and collected river clay in baskets, and brought it back to the pottery yard. They cleaned the clay, removing all the stones, and then pummelled it to make it soft and smooth. Then, very nervously, Laxman slapped on a handful of clay on the wheel and began to make pots. He was still not too good, and many times the pots came out all twisted, and that made Parvati laugh.

Still, enough pots came out right; they were dried in the sun and baked on a fire in the kiln. One evening the three of them stacked the pottery into the bullock cart and took them to the shop in the market. The shopkeeper bought all of them. It felt so good to earn money.

They were heading back when they heard the thudding of horses' hooves, and six horsemen came galloping down the road in a cloud of dust and swept past their bullock cart.

'Soldiers!' Parvati exclaimed. 'Where are they going?'

'Look! They are going into the vihara.'

They parked the cart outside and Laxman ran to the gate. He found it was shut. 'This gate is never closed!' he remarked.

'Let's go in from the back gate.' Parvati hopped down from the cart and began running. Soon they had found their way into the vihara.

In the quadrangle, the monks were milling about looking anxious and whispering to each other. They saw that the soldiers were huddled at the door of Prior Bhadraka's room, talking urgently. They ran to find Aditya, and entering his room, they stopped at the door in shock. Aditya lay on a palette on the floor, his eyes closed. A bandage was tied around his head and there were patches of blood on his robe.

The monk who was tending to Aditya turned and said, 'Out! Don't disturb him!'

Hearts thudding, eyes wide with panic, they came out and asked another monk, 'What happened? How did Aditya get hurt?'

The young bhikkhu had tears in his eyes. 'He was trying to protect Bhikkhu Rakshita, and those men hit him with sticks!'

'Robbers?'

'No no … not robbers … they have kidnapped Rakshita!'

'Kidnapped a monk?' they stared in surprise. 'Why?'

'That is what we can't understand. They did not steal anything, not even the gold and silver bowls in the chaitya. And now the king has heard of it and sent the soldiers. Only Aditya knows what happened, and he is unconscious.'

Just then they spotted a familiar figure at the Prior's door. 'General Shilaka! What's he doing here? Did the king send him?'

The monk stared at them. 'Rakshita is his son; don't you know that? As it is, he was unhappy that his son had joined the sangha, and now he is blaming the vihara for putting his son's life in danger.'

They were startled by the sound of loud drumming at the gate and turned to look. They saw that a dark, stocky man had come riding in, followed by a dozen soldiers.

'Oh, Sakyamuni!' the monk remembered the Buddha in panic. 'What's *he* doing here?'

'Who?'

'The king!'

'Oooh … I have never seen the king before!' Parvati had gone quite breathless in excitement.

They stared, fascinated, as Ashoka sprang down from the horse. He was of medium height, wearing an antariya

wrapped around his legs and a short sleeveless jacket. His long hair was tied in a knot at his shoulder but he was not wearing a turban. Laxman noticed the dagger tucked into his belt. Parvati studied the dusky, high cheek-boned face, the large eyes and firm lips. The king wore little jewellery, just gold earrings and bracelets.

'Now I've seen the king,' she thought, 'and he's not very handsome, is he?'

As the king strode past them, everyone bent their heads in respect. Bhadraka and Shilaka came hurrying up and bowed before King Ashoka. Shilaka, who was looking anxious and upset, said something to the king, and Ashoka put a hand on his shoulder and the three men walked inside.

Another monk standing nearby said, 'The general must have complained to the king. He did not like it when his son joined the sangha.'

'Does the general not have faith?'

'No. He worships the old gods and goddesses. Our king gives us the freedom to follow any faith we like.'

Just then a soldier came up and asked all visitors to leave. The children had come out of the gate when Laxman suddenly stopped in his tracks and said, 'We should get Vaidji immediately. Only he can help Aditya.'

***

An hour later the children and the old vaid stood at the closed gate of the vihara as a soldier stared at them suspiciously. 'No one's allowed inside.'

Vaidji said calmly, 'I have medicine for the injured monk Bhikkhu Aditya. You can check with Prior Bhadraka. I am the physician at this vihara. Tell him that Vaid Nagasena is here.'

As the soldier went inside, Parvati crinkled her nose and looked up at the old man. 'I didn't know your name is Nagasena.'

'Sometimes I forget it too, because you all keep calling me Vaidji.' There was an amused twinkle in his eyes.

A novice monk came hurrying out to escort them to Aditya's room. Peering through the door, they saw Nagasena open his bundle of herbs and roots and small pots of powder. He made a paste, and after cleaning the wound on Aditya's head, he put the paste on the deep cut and then wrapped a bandage on it. He lit a small stick of incense and blew the smoke on Aditya's face, and that made him cough. There was a murmur of relief as Aditya slowly opened his eyes and then looked blankly around him.

'Can you hear me?' Nagasena, bending over Aditya, asked, and the monk nodded weakly. 'Can you see?' Aditya nodded again. 'Jai Ma Durga!' sighed Nagasena in relief. 'You'll live, my friend.' He turned to a monk. 'Get me a bowl of milk with saffron and sugar in it.' He fed Aditya, who was soon asleep. 'He'll talk tomorrow. Now all of you leave the room. I'll stay with him tonight.'

Next morning when they went to the vihara, they saw that Aditya was asleep and Nagasena had gone home. They found the vaid sitting in the verandah of his thatched hut.

The old man was slowly munching some puffed rice mixed with mustard oil, chopped onions and cucumbers. The children sat down beside him and aimed their questions at his expressionless face.

'Vaidji, is he talking?'

Nagasena popped another handful of puffed rice into his mouth and chewed slowly.

'Did he sleep last night?'

Nagasena went on chewing.

'Can we see him?'

Nagasena chewed on for a while and then said, 'He'll live.'

'What did he say? Who attacked him?'

'I'll tell you after I've finished eating. I can't talk and eat at the same time.'

'Ohhh … really, Vaidji!' Parvati glared at him.

'Patience, girl! It looks like you three have had no breakfast. So have some …' and they were handed another bowl of puffed rice and cucumbers. Grumbling away, they began to eat.

'Ohhh … you eat so slowly!' they commented on Nagasena's chewing.

'I only have ten teeth left.'

Then finally Nagasena told them all that Aditya had told him.

The night he was attacked, Aditya and Rakshita were in the chaitya. Aditya was teaching the novice monk how to meditate, so they were sitting with their eyes closed, when suddenly four men entered the hall. They were holding knives and sticks and had masked their faces with their turbans. Aditya thought they wanted to steal the gold and silver bowls and ornaments that stood on the altar, but to his surprise, the men began to drag Rakshita away.

As Aditya tried to save him, one man shouted, 'That's Aditya! Hit him! He has to die.' Two men attacked him with sticks. Luckily for him, hearing the noise, the other monks came running into the chaitya. By then the men had dragged Rakshita away, and Aditya had lost consciousness.

'They wanted to kill Aditya?'

Nagasena nodded.

'Why?'

Nagasena shook his head. 'I don't know. I think these men have kidnapped Rakshita because he is the son of a rich man. They will now ask for a ransom to free him. They knew that a vihara is not guarded, and it would be easy to kidnap him.'

'Have they asked for a ransom yet?'

'No, not so far.' Nagasena studied their anxious faces. 'How do you three know Aditya?'

'We became friends when he began coming to our lane to beg. We like listening to him. He tells such wonderful stories.'

'He's also a very good teacher,' Nagasena said. 'Ask him to teach you to read and write.'

The three exchanged a quick glance, and Laxman shrugged. 'We're shudras, remember?'

Nakul gave a slight bitter smile. 'Ballabh says we cannot touch books. They are only for Brahmins.'

'Ballabh is a fat fool. I'm a Brahmin too, and as soon as you can read, you can come and read my books.'

'Actually,' Laxman grinned, 'Aditya is teaching us. We can read whole sentences now.'

'Good ... good ... don't stop.' Nagasena got up slowly. He looked very tired. 'Now help me. I have to make more ointment and a syrup for Aditya.' He gave his sweet toothless smile. 'Get to work!'

Laxman ran about fetching the jars and bottles, Parvati picked fresh herbs from the back garden, Nakul cleaned the stone mortar and pestle. 'I think I'll train you three to become my assistants,' Nagasena laughed. 'You'll do all the work and I'll make all the money.'

'Hah! No money, no work!' Parvati said, busy chopping the herbs. 'I expect to be paid.'

'I'm sure you do!'

'Aditya is your friend, Vaidji?'

'Yes he is. I'm getting old, and so I'm teaching him about herbs so he can make the medicines and become the physician at the vihara.' Nagasena sniffed at a bowl of powder and then carefully measured a small spoonful into the earthen jar. 'And he lends me books from their library to read. Their guru, this Gautama Buddha, was a clever man and said many useful things.'

'So you worship the Sakyamuni too?' Nakul asked.

'No, I prefer Ma Durga,' he grinned. 'I like fighting goddesses.'

'And Aditya doesn't mind?'

'Why should he?' Nagasena looked puzzled. 'After all, the Buddha and Ma Durga have no problems with each other.' And he roared with laughter. 'One prays and the other fights!'

After staying up all night and making the medicines, the old man was tired, so he gave the ointment and syrup to the children with long instructions. 'Tell the monk taking care of Aditya that he has to put the ointment on the wound twice a day, but only after cleaning it. He has to add this syrup to milk and give it to him thrice a day. It will give him energy. He has to eat lots of green leafy vegetables, lightly boiled, with no spices, and thin dal with rice.' He frowned at them. 'Can you remember all that?'

Nakul grinned. 'Parvati will.'

At the vihara they were relieved to find Aditya sitting up in bed. Parvati stood by Aditya's bed and repeated Nagasena's instructions word by word, making Aditya smile. 'Didn't forget a word, did you?' Then, as they were leaving, he said, 'Oh, I nearly forgot! Will you give this to Nagasena?' From under his pillow he pulled out a few beads hanging from a thread and a square silver pendant. 'One of the robbers was wearing this and I must have pulled it off him when I was fighting him. I found it in my hand when I woke up.'

Nakul studied the beads. 'Looks like it's from a necklace.'

'Maybe the three of you and Nagasena can discover who was wearing it. That pendant is rather unusual.'

Parvati tied the beads and pendant to the end of her uttariya as Laxman asked, 'Any news of Bhikkhu Rakshita?'

Aditya shook his head. 'Not a word, and it's very odd. Why did they take him away if they didn't want a ransom?'

When they got to Nagasena, he stared at the pendant and said, 'Clearly my friend Aditya is still not thinking clearly. I'm a physician, not a jeweller. I know about herbs, not about jewellery. Go find a jeweller.'

'Where?' Laxman asked. 'And why would he answer our questions?'

Nagasena sighed and then limped out into the courtyard and pointed across the road to a row of shops. 'See that shop with the blue awnings? That is the shop of a jeweller. He comes to me for medicines. Go and tell him I have sent you.'

The jeweller, sitting on a thick mattress on the floor, leaning against a bolster, studied the pendant and said, 'Nagasena wants a pendant like this?'

'I'm not sure …' Nakul stumbled a bit in his explanation. 'I mean … he just told us to show you this and ask if anyone bought it from you.'

The man shook his head. 'I haven't made this, but they are available everywhere. Soldiers often buy these pendants.'

'*Soldiers*?' Parvati asked, surprised.

'These are lucky charms. We put a small piece of cloth with a prayer written on it inside the pendant and soldiers wear it when they go off to war. They think the mantra protects them from the enemy.'

They went back to Nagasena and when he heard what the jeweller had said, he stood up. 'Soldiers, eh? Aditya has to hear this. Let's go!' Then he gave a dramatic sigh. 'Oof! All the walking! You children are making me work so hard!'

Parvati slipped her hand into his and smiled at him. 'Vaidji, I promise I'll press your legs when we get back.'

'For free?' the old man smiled down at her gentle face.

'Of course!'

***

It was getting dark and Aditya's room was lit up by the wavering light of a small earthen lamp, filling the room with shadows.

'Soldiers?' Aditya was sitting up now. 'Why would soldiers kidnap a general's son? If they were caught, they would die for it.'

'Soldiers are trained to obey orders,' Nagasena said softly, 'without asking any questions.'

Aditya stared at his old friend and a wordless message seemed to be moving between the two men. 'And they were ordered to kill me.'

'And the monks would be blamed for not protecting Rakshita.'

'And His Majesty would be unhappy with this vihara ...'

'And Rakshita would be removed from the monastery.'

Finally Laxman protested. 'I don't understand what you two are saying!'

'Soldiers will always obey their general. These soldiers were ordered by their general to kidnap Rakshita and kill Aditya.'

'Which general?' Parvati frowned.

'Think!' Nagasena said.

'Of course!' Nakul nodded broodingly. 'General Shilaka! Remember what we heard that evening, when he was shouting at Prior Bhadraka? He was furious that his son had become a monk, and he blamed Aditya.'

'Clever boy!'

'And now everyone blames the vihara for not protecting Rakshita.'

'Clever girl!'

The children kept quiet as Nagasena and Aditya brooded and slowly worked it all out.

Aditya said, 'No one will believe us.'

'They will say, how can a father kidnap his own son?' Nagasena nodded.

'And Shilaka is a very powerful man.'

'We have no proof.'

'The only way to get proof is to find out where they are hiding the boy.'

'How do we do that?'

'How should I know? I only know about herbs and potions.' Nagasena shrugged. 'You are the clever one, Aditya. Think!'

Aditya lay back with a sigh. 'Nagasena, now you've given me a headache.'

***

Next morning the children entered Nagasena's home carrying a basket of small earthen jars. 'Baba sent these for you,' Parvati said. 'You can use them to keep your powders and pastes.'

'Your Baba is a good man!' Nagasena looked delighted. He was tending his herb garden and soon the children were helping him dig the soil and water the plants. They all looked up as two soldiers rode past. 'There is a lot of excitement in Shilaka's house today. Wonder what's happening.'

Nakul looked up. 'Does Shilaka live here?'

'Yes, down the lane.'

Laxman stood still. 'The second house on the left?'

'That's right.'

'A few days back I saw Ballabh go in there.'

Nagasena frowned. 'I've never seen Ballabh here before.'

The three children exchanged thoughtful glances. 'Do you think Ballabh knows something?'

***

That afternoon the children were loitering aimlessly in the lane outside the temple. Laxman's plan was to keep a watch on what Ballabh did and follow him if he left the temple, but so far he had stayed inside.

'It's so hot!' Parvati protested. 'Let's go home.'

Just then Ballabh came hurrying out and nearly crashed into Laxman. He stopped himself just in time. He was holding a roll of cloth in one hand. 'Oh! What are you doing here?'

'Nothing!'

Ballabh stared thoughtfully at them. 'You all go to the vihara, don't you?' Laxman nodded. 'How is that injured monk? Aditya, isn't that his name?'

'He's fine.'

'Does he remember who attacked him?'

Nakul shook his head. 'He can't remember anything,' he replied while wondering why Ballabh was so interested.

Ballabh looked up at the sky and the glaring sun. His face was already dripping with sweat. He asked them, 'Can you do something for me?'

'What?' Laxman asked suspiciously.

Ballabh held out the roll of cloth. 'Can you take this letter to my client? He lives near the market.'

Just then his wife Vedavati came out and said, 'You should go yourself. It's an important letter, you know …'

'Oh, it's so hot, and it takes so long to walk to the general's house!' He didn't notice how the three children had suddenly become still.

'Which general?' Parvati asked carefully.

'Shilaka. You have to go past Vaid Nagasena's house. It's the second house on the left.'

'Sure, we can do that,' Nakul nodded solemnly. 'How much will you pay?'

'Oh *really*!' Ballabh dropped a single pana coin in Nakul's hand. 'But hurry! He is waiting for this letter.'

As they walked away, they heard Vedavati protest again. 'I really think you should have gone …'

'Oh, what's the problem? They can't read!'

The three of them turned the corner and went behind a big banyan tree. Laxman carefully opened the roll of cloth and read slowly.

The daughter of the mountains keeps him safe on her waters. If you seek him, come to the palace of the white pillars.

'Huh?' Parvati rolled her eyes.

'What does this mean?' Nakul brooded.

'It's some sort of a code.' Laxman rolled the cloth and tied it up. 'We'd better deliver this first and then we'll ask Vaidji.'

They ran, panting, to the mansion of Shilaka, and were stopped at the gate by two guards. What made them even more breathless was that one of the men was wearing a necklace exactly like the one that Aditya had given them.

'This is a letter for General Shilaka from Ballabh pandit at the temple.' The soldier did not ask any questions, just took the letter and waved them away.

They ran to Nagasena's house and found that he had gone to the vihara, and soon three panting children burst into Aditya's room.

'Ballabh's sending coded messages to the general!' Parvati exclaimed.

'He knows something,' Nakul said.

'The soldier at the gate was wearing a necklace exactly like the one Bhikkhu Aditya had found, Vaidji!' Laxman said excitedly.

'Slowly ... slowly ...' Nagasena raised a patient hand as the children tried to calm their thumping hearts and told them about the message.

Aditya threw back his head and laughed. 'Oh Sakyamuni! He thought you couldn't read!' And then he turned to Parvati. 'Let's hear the message, my parrot girl.'

Parvati gathered her wits about her, closed her eyes, took a deep breath and recited the words.

The daughter of the mountains keeps him safe on her waters. If you seek him, come to the palace of the white pillars.'

Then she shrugged. 'Of course, I don't have a clue what that means.'

'Daughter of the mountains?' Aditya stared at Nagasena. 'Who's she?'

'Oh you bhikkhus! You know nothing!' Nagasena shook his head. 'The Ganga river, of course! She is the daughter of the Himalayas.'

'He is safe on her waters ...' Laxman muttered and then shouted, 'Of course! They must be keeping Rakshita a prisoner on a boat!'

'But there are hundreds of boats on the Ganga!' Nakul protested.

'But there is only one palace with white pillars by the river,' Aditya said. 'It's that old broken-down mansion by the last ghat. The place is usually deserted.' He stood up and went to the door and called out to a monk to get a chariot. 'I have to tell Bhadraka about this and then I'll have to go to the king. We are monks, we cannot fight soldiers, and only the king can order the army to act against Shilaka.' He quickly wrapped a cloth around his shoulders and began to walk out of his cell. 'You all wait for me here at the vihara.'

Nagasena and the children stood at the gate and watched Aditya and Bhadraka drive away. Then Laxman said, 'Wait here? Huh! I refuse to wait. So do we go to the ghat by bullock cart? Or do we walk?'

Nagasena laughed. 'Bullock cart is a good idea, Laxman! My old knees tell me that it's too far to walk.'

Soon the potter's cart with Laxman holding the reins was creaking along the road when they heard the sound of horses, and two chariots and a dozen horsemen went galloping past them.

As a familiar face flashed past, Parvati said excitedly, 'Oh! Did you see? Wasn't that the king?'

'Laxman, hurry up!' Nagasena said.

'We're nearly there.'

A little later they were sitting in the cart near the river ghat, watching all the action as if they were watching a play. Aditya and Bhadraka were there too. Ashoka sprang down from his chariot and led the soldiers away. They were all ready with their swords.

'I thought the king does not fight anymore, ever since he joined the Buddhist sangha.'

'He does not attack anymore. Of course he will fight crime and evil,' Nagasena said with a satisfied sigh. 'Why do you think we still have a standing army? If anyone attacks Magadha, he'll smash them to pieces.'

The door of the mansion was broken down with a large log of wood and they rushed inside. Soon the soldiers came out dragging some men, and among them they saw a familiar fat figure.

'That's Ballabh!'

There was a boat parked in the river behind the mansion and Aditya began running towards it. He soon came out holding a tired-looking Rakshita and helped him onto the chariot. By then Ashoka and the soldiers had galloped away with their prisoners, and the chariot followed behind.

'Where are they going now?' Nagasena asked Aditya.

'To catch Shilaka.'

'So I was right,' Nagasena said with a satisfied smile. 'It was a father kidnapping his own son.'

'Are you always right?' Parvati wanted to know.

'Pretty much!' And the satisfied smile on Nagasena's face made the children burst out laughing.

'All this excitement makes you hungry,' Nakul said with a satisfied burp.

It was night and they were all having a meal in the vihara as Aditya and Nagasena answered all their questions.

'Why was Ballabh helping Shilaka?'

'Because he hates the vihara,' Nagasena replied. 'The monks welcome everyone—rich and poor, men and women, and people of every caste, and everyone is treated equally. They don't demand money for every prayer and they don't hold expensive religious rituals like the Brahmin priests do. Many people now follow the Sakyamuni and no longer go to the temple and pay for pujas. Ballabh was losing money, and you know how greedy he is.'

'And the monks teach children to read,' Parvati gave a cheeky grin.

'By the way, the king has announced a reward for you three and Nagasena for solving the mystery of the kidnapping.'

'What is the reward?' Laxman the businessman wanted to know.

Aditya scratched his head. 'He told me but I forget … I think he said five hundred panas …'

'Really, Aditya!' Even Nagasena looked irritated.

Aditya threw up his hands. 'I'm a monk, Nagasena! You know we're not allowed to touch money.'

A month later, Laxman and Nakul's families stood before the altar in the chaitya wearing their best clothes, as Aditya welcomed them as new followers of the Sakyamuni, Gautama Buddha. Nagasena sat in the front row watching them with a smile. Aditya had asked him if he would also join the ceremonies. Nagasena had said no, thank you, he liked gods and goddesses and only wanted to worship his beautiful fighting goddess, Durga.

……………………

HISTORICAL NOTE

Gautama Buddha preached his compassionate and humane faith in the 6th century BCE and for a thousand years Buddhism was a popular religion in India. The main reason for his popularity was that he rejected the caste system and said everyone was born equal. So people of the lower castes like craftspeople and traders became Buddhists. The Brahmin priests forced people to perform expensive religious rituals and animal sacrifices and they held on to knowledge by stopping poor people from being educated. The Buddhists had no rituals, and the monks encouraged people to get educated. Hindu women had no rights and were never educated, but many Buddhist nuns wrote poetry that was collected in a book called the *Therigatha*. People trusted the monks like Aditya who were kind and helpful and led simple lives.

....

THE PRINCESS OF BEANS

Madhura's long fingers hovered thoughtfully over the basket of flowers for a moment. Then she picked a jasmine and a marigold, swiftly wove them into the garland and then picked a deep red rose, sniffing happily at its fragrance. Madhura was making a garland for her favourite god, Lord Vishnu. Every morning the first garland she made was always for Him.

She was sitting in her mother's flower shop, a small space with a thatched roof held up by bamboo poles, piled with baskets of flowers and bowls of incense. Their shop was the busiest in the street because it was closest to the gate of the

Vaikuntha Perumal Temple in the royal city of Kanchipuram. This was the newest and biggest temple in the city that had been built recently by their king Nandi Varman, and the stone walls and pillars had beautiful carvings.

The tall gopuram gateway led inside to a beautiful shrine where, in the sanctum, stood Lord Vaikuntha Perumal, or Lord Vishnu, the king of the universe. He was clad in golden garments, glittering with precious jewels, and wearing a tall gold crown. He had a gentle smile on his lips.

Her mother had taught her to always string the first garland of the day for Lord Vishnu. As she said often to Madhura, their livelihood depended on many pilgrims coming to worship at the temple. Madhura liked to think that the garlands she made were all laid at his feet. Every morning she and her mother came to the shop with baskets of brightly-coloured flowers—red and pink roses, creamy white jasmines, orange marigolds, also bunches of tulsi and banana leaves. They sat at the shop and threaded the flowers and leaves into fragrant garlands. Pilgrims going into the temple bought a basket of garlands, rose petals, incense sticks and an earthen lamp that they offered to the god.

The shouts of the palace guards made her look up. 'Here comes the princess,' Madhura said to herself, eagerly leaning forward to look at her. 'She is early today.'

As she watched, her eyes bright with interest, the pretty young Princess Jayalakshmi got out of her palanquin and came walking slowly down the narrow lane. As always, she was going to the temple for her morning puja. Madhura's hands lay still, holding a half-strung garland as she sat mesmerized, staring at the royal procession. The palace guards came first, carrying shiny spears and wearing tall turbans. Behind them the princess came strolling along, surrounded by her companions, and they were followed by a row of maids carrying large silver platters filled with flowers, sweets, fruits and incense.

Madhura carefully studied what the princess wore that morning—a long skirt in green silk embroidered in gold and a short blouse. She wore a golden veil sheer as gossamer around her shoulders. Madhura was nine and she guessed that the princess was twelve or thirteen.

Madhura stared at the princess' gold necklace that was made of a row of tiny pendants shaped like mangoes and set with red rubies. 'What a pretty necklace!' she thought in wonder. Then she took a closer look at Jayalakshmi's face and thought like she did every time she saw her, 'Why doesn't she ever smile?'

As Princess Jayalakshmi swept past, she did not notice the little girl in the flower shop who watched her with such wide-eyed admiration. Madhura would have been thrilled if the princess had smiled at her, but she never even looked her way. Princesses were too important to notice poor garland girls.

'Amma,' Madhura turned to look at her mother, 'why is the princess coming to the temple every day? She never did before.'

'She is to be married soon,' her mother replied as she sold a garland to a customer and then counted the coins. 'I heard that her mother, our Queen Rajyalakshmi, wants her to do the puja for a month. She is praying to Lord Vaikuntha Perumal for a happy married life and lots of sons.'

'I wish she would come to our shop,' Madhura said dreamily. 'I'd weave a special garland for her, made only of jasmines and red roses.'

Her mother looked at her dreamy face and laughed. 'Stop dreaming, child! She is Princess Jayalakshmi, daughter of King Nandi Varman of the great Pallava dynasty. They have gardens in the palace and maids to string garlands. She would never come to our shop for flowers.'

'Why not? Aren't our garlands pretty?' Madhura frowned.

'It's not that. It is because we are poor,' her mother's eyes were gentle as she looked at her wide-eyed daughter. 'The rich and powerful do not notice poor people like us. They just walk past like the princess does. They never see our faces, they never talk to us ...'

'Why not?'

'I don't know. You'll have to ask a princess one day.'

'She wears such pretty clothes and jewellery,' Madhura looked down at her simple blue cotton skirt all faded after many washes, 'but have you noticed, Amma, she never smiles?'

'Maybe princesses are not supposed to smile.' Her mother's quick laugh told Madhura that she was teasing her. 'You'll have to ask her that too.'

Madhura tied a string of jasmines around her hair and said briskly, 'Clothes … jewellery … palanquins … dosais and payasam to eat every day … If I were a princess, I would smile all the time!'

Later, while her hands were busy stringing together the garlands, her head was busy with thoughts. 'The princess is so lucky! She wears a new dress every day and even changes her jewellery. She has maids to do all her work and friends to play with. And she must eat such delicious meals—the best rice cooked in ghee, fresh fish from the sea and desserts like payasam filled with raisins.'

She thought of the small thatched hut in which they lived, with its bare brick walls and hard earthen floor on which they slept on thin woven mats. 'In the palace she must have a big room, a soft bed and a pool to bathe in. She wouldn't have to walk to the river to bathe.'

That evening Madhura and her younger brother Sivaraman waited for their father to come back from work. He was a weaver and worked in one of the workshops that made silk saris for the royal household. Then, as the family sat down to eat their simple dinner of rice, sambar beans, peas and a coconut dessert dish, Madhura said suddenly, 'If I were a princess, I would never eat beans.'

Her father gave her a startled look. 'Who's a princess?'

'Madhura has been watching the Princess Jayalakshmi every day,' her mother explained. 'I think she wants to be one too.'

'If you become a princess, I'll be a prince!' her brother said with a wide grin. 'Prince Sivaraman! I'll ride a horse and fight with a sword,' he waved his arm. 'Wonderful!'

As the others began to laugh, Madhura said stubbornly, 'What's wrong with wanting to be a princess? I'm sure she is the happiest person in the world!'

'Aren't you happy?' her mother studied her face and asked curiously. 'I thought you are.'

'I would be, Amma, if you were a queen!' Madhura explained patiently, widening her eyes. Mothers never did understand, did they? Everything had to be explained to them. 'The princess is so lucky she has Queen Rajyalakshmi as a mother! The queen buys her silks and jewels and she never walks in the sun. She always travels in a palanquin. And she doesn't have to make …' Then she stopped, noticing a sudden flash of sadness in her Amma's eyes, and went back to eating.

'Ah!' said her father solemnly, 'so it is all your Amma's fault!'

'Ummm … not really, Appa …' Madhura took a quick look at her mother's bent head and then had to admit, 'Amma can't really help it.'

'Then stop dreaming of being a princess,' her mother said firmly. 'What is so bad about your life, will you tell me? Why do you want to be a princess?'

'If I were a princess, I wouldn't have to eat beans. That is why!' Madhura revealed, holding up a handful of beans and coconut. 'We have beans all the time and I just, absolutely and totally, hate beans!'

'Aha!' her father nodded. 'Now I understand! It's all about *beans*!' and the look in his eyes told her that her Appa was not going to let her forget this. She was right. He grinned at his wife and announced teasingly, 'Our princess Madhura hates beans! Remember that! No beans in this house!'

'What about me?' asked Sivaraman plaintively. 'I *like* beans, Appa!'

From then on, her father and Sivaraman began to call her the Princess of Beans and it made Madhura absolutely hopping mad. 'No one understands me,' she brooded, sitting gloomily in the flower shop. 'They just know how to tease and laugh. What is so wrong about wanting to be a princess?'

***

One morning, a few days later, as the princess was going past, Madhura turned to look at her mother and discovered that she was busy at the back of the shop. She crept out and followed the royal entourage into the temple. They entered an open courtyard and then walked through a pillared corridor that led to the main shrine where the priests stood at the door to welcome the princess. They led her inside to the sanctum where the image of Lord Vaikuntha Perumal stood, surrounded by the golden glow of tall brass lamps and wreathed in incense smoke.

'Will she pray at all the three sanctums?' wondered Madhura, because this was a very special temple. There were three sanctums, one on top of the other, with three different images of Lord Vishnu. On the ground floor the god was sitting on a throne like a king, on the first floor Lord Vishnu was standing and blessing everybody, and on the second he was reclining, as if taking rest. Madhura liked the standing image the most as she thought it had the kindest face.

A small crowd had gathered to watch. The royal guards pushed them back roughly and made them stand in the hallway. Madhura stood on her toes and managed to catch a glimpse of the princess standing before the god holding a handful of flowers as the priest raised the many-flamed arati lamp and began to chant the mantras. Madhura leaned against the cool stone of a pillar and looked around happily. She liked temples with their air smelling of incense and flowers, the clang of bells and the raised voices singing mantras. There were images of Lord Vishnu and other gods and goddesses everywhere, carved on the pillars and placed in niches of the walls.

'So when is the wedding?' a man spoke next to Madhura and she turned to see the two royal guards standing on the other side of the pillar.

'Next month. Our princess is going far, all the way to Thanjavur.' Madhura's ears perked up and she crept closer to listen.

'I hear the queen is not happy about the princess being married into the royal family of Thanjavur.'

'And neither is the princess.'

'But what can they do? The king decides and the queen and the princess have to obey.'

'They say the Thanjavur prince is much older than our princess and already has two wives and three children. Our princess will only be a junior queen.'

'Poor little princess! I heard from a maid that she cries often and is also scared of going so far away. She's only thirteen!'

'But she will have to obey His Majesty.'

A thoughtful Madhura wandered slowly to the shop. Later, when the princess went past on her way back to the palace, she looked at her sad face and thought, 'Oh poor princess! Thanjavur is so far away! She may not come back to Kanchipuram for a long time.' Her heart thudded with sympathy. 'Imagine going so far away all alone and then not seeing your Amma and Appa for years ...'

***

That evening Madhura was helping her mother cook dinner while her father and Sivaraman were lounging around, watching them and cracking bad jokes. As she chopped a pumpkin, she said, 'When the princess came to do puja in the temple this morning, I followed her.'

'Oh, that's where you went!' Her mother turned to look at her. 'I was looking for you. Next time tell me before you leave.'

'What was the princess doing?' Sivaraman wanted to know.

'I saw her do puja and then I heard two palace guards talking. They said the princess will have to go to Thanjavur after her marriage.'

Her mother was busy cleaning a plate of rice, carefully picking out small stones and pieces of husk. She raised her head and widened her eyes in this very dramatic way, as if she was worried. 'Oh no! Now do you want to follow her and get married and live in Thanjavur too?'

'No, Amma, I don't,' Madhura said patiently. Why didn't adults ever let her finish what she was saying? 'I don't want to ever leave Kanchi.' Then she added with a small smile, 'Unless you come with me.'

Her mother gave her a thoughtful look. 'How can I! You'll be a married woman. Do you think the queen will go with the princess?'

'I know she won't, but then won't the princess miss her?'

'Of course she will. And that is why I'm going to marry you to a boy who lives right here in Kanchi. So I can see you whenever I want.'

'What if Appa wants to send me far away?' asked Madhura anxiously, remembering what the guard said about the queen and the princess having to obey the king.

Her Amma turned to glare at her Appa. 'Just let him try!'

Her father shrugged. 'I always obey your Amma. Don't you know that? So I promise to find you a boy in Kanchi and also make sure your mother-in-law never cooks beans.'

'Here we go again!' Madhura sat up straight and glared at him. 'Appa, can't you think of anything except *beans*?'

'How can I?' his grin widened. 'As your father, I'm the king of beans, remember? And your mother is the queen ...' So saying, her Amma, Appa and Sivaraman laughed so much, Madhura wanted to hit them. Instead, she put her head in her hands and pretended to weep, and that made them all laugh even more.

That night, over dinner, her father had some exciting news to share. That day a royal minister had come into the weavers' workshop and bought all the saris for the princess' wedding. So all the weavers were given a special bonus of a month's salary. The next evening Madhura's father would take them all shopping.

'I want a red skirt,' said Madhura, very excited, 'with a golden border.'

'Can I buy some marbles?' asked Sivaraman. He added optimistically, 'And a catapult too?'

'Do you think we have money to buy a new rice pot?' her mother wondered. 'A brass one?'

'Yes!' smiled her father. 'And we'll get new thatch for the roof and maybe build another room. I'm feeling rich today!'

'Then we'll also have dosais at the food shop,' her mother said happily, 'and I won't have to cook.'

'And a bowl of payasam too!' added Sivaraman with a grin.

That night, lying on her mat, Madhura dreamed happily about red skirts and marbles, dosais and payasam, jasmines and roses ... then, as she was about to fall asleep, she thought, 'It's not all that bad being the princess of beans.'

....

A HISTORICAL NOTE

The beautiful Vaikuntha Perumal Temple still stands in Kanchipuram in Tamil Nadu. It was built over twelve hundred years ago by the Pallava king, Nandi Varman II. It is one the oldest temples of India where worship has continued uninterrupted since the eighth century. This story is fictional, and Princess Jayalakshmi and Madhura, the flower girl, are imaginary characters. I did buy a basket of flowers there, at the temple gate, from a smiling little girl with big, dark eyes and pink ribbons in her curly hair. She is my Madhura.

....

A STRANGER IN VIJAYANAGAR

As the mantras rose in the air, the mridangam drums played, and Ambika, the devadasi, danced. I watched the two men whispering to each other.

Every evening, for the last three days, the two men had stood there among the crowd watching the temple arati, and what had caught my eye was that they did not bother to actually watch the ceremonies. They did not join in the singing or pray with folded hands or even watch Ambika. All they did was whisper conspiratorially into each other's ears for a while and then go away even before the arati was over. Somehow it made me very uneasy.

Laying down the bell that I had been clanging to the beat of the mridangams, I slid quietly into the crowd. Trying to move casually, I pushed in deeper until I had edged my way to a spot right behind the two men. Then, leaning forward, I tried to hear what they were saying.

I discovered that eavesdropping wasn't easy. The high-ceilinged mandapam, the sanctum hall of the Pampa Temple, was echoing to the sound of the arati. There was the raised voice of my father, the temple priest, loudly chanting mantras to the sound of ringing bells and blowing conches. His chanting got louder as he raised the many-flamed brass lamp before the image of the Goddess Pampa Devi. Then there were the two musicians playing the mridangam drum and flute and the deep jingle of the anklets of Ambika as she whirled and swayed before the goddess. It was all leading to quite an uproar.

All I could catch were snatches of conversation that made no sense at all. The tall, thin man with the hooked nose said, '... at the site of the new temple ... will go and try to find out tomorrow ...'

Then the conches blew and I could hear nothing more.

After a while, the short, plump man said, 'Are you sure the king will come?' The tall man nodded.

The fat man seemed to ask a question and the tall man muttered, 'By the North Road, it takes five days by horse ...'

By then the arati was over. The music died as Ambika ended her dance with a deep pranam, and in the sudden silence the men stopped talking as everyone bent to the ground before the Goddess in prayer. I too touched my forehead to the floor, mumbled a prayer, and when I looked up again, the two men were gone.

***

Next morning while helping my father around the temple, all I could think of was the conversation I had overheard. The new temple, the tall man had said. I wondered if it was the temple I went to nearly every day. Our king, the great Krishna Deva Raya of Vijayanagar, was building a new temple for Lord Krishna on a hill near the ancient Virupaksha temple. Everyone said it was going to be the greatest temple ever built, and I agreed. I was watching the beautiful work the stone carvers and sculptors were doing at the temple site.

That was my only dream, to work as a sculptor. I did not want to be a priest like my father, memorising mantras and reading horoscopes. I draw and sketch all the time, with a stick on the dust and on walls with a piece of charcoal. But I don't want to paint—I dream of being a stone carver. To be out there with those large stones, hammer and chisel in hand, carving out gods and elephants, chariots and flying apsaras on the walls and pillars of temples! It was stupid of me to dream, because whoever had heard of a Brahmin priest's son becoming a sculptor?

Still, whenever I had some free time, I went to watch the men at work at the site of the new temple. That morning, as I was about to leave, my younger sister Manjira came running after me, calling, 'Devayya, can I come with you please?'

As we were climbing the hill strewn with red gold boulders, I could already hear that lovely "chink chink" of the iron hammer hitting the chisel. As we got closer, I could see the rows of men bent over long pieces of stone, carving them into beautiful pillars. Chips of stone were flying around their bent heads.

Finding a spot in the shade of a half-built gateway, Manjira and I sat down to watch a boy my age smoothening out a rough slab of stone with slow careful slicing of the chisel.

He looked up and smiled at us. 'I see you here often. Do you like our work?'

'I wish I could carve like you. I'm Devayya. This is my sister Manjira.'

'I'm Ballava,' said the boy, stopping work to sharpen the edge of his chisel on a wet piece of stone. 'My father is the chief sculptor here. You could ask him to take you on as a student.'

I just shook my head as I knew my father would never allow me to leave the temple where men belonging to our family had been priests for generations.

Just then Manjira interrupted my gloomy thoughts. 'It looks like you have another guest today, Ballava.' I turned to look, and felt my heart thud. I had seen that man before. It was the tall, thin man with the hooked nose. So I had guessed right—this was the temple he had been talking about! Noticing the surprise on my face, Manjira asked, 'What's the matter? Do you know that man, Devayya?'

'Yes, he was there at the Pampa Temple. There is Fat Man, and this one is Hooked Nose …' and I told them about how they had come to the temple to talk, and what I had overheard. 'I wonder what he wants.'

'Do you think he is a thief?' Manjira asked breathlessly.

'What's there to steal here?' Ballava laughed and said, 'Unless he wants chunks of stone.' All the while the man I had begun calling Hooked Nose was wandering around, chatting with the workmen. After a while, with a polite namaskar, he turned and walked away. Watching him go, Ballava said, 'Well, now you have got me curious too. Let's go and find out what he was asking my father.'

Ballava's father Chinappa was busy carving a dancing woman holding a drum, carefully adding a flowery pattern to her skirt. He looked up as we sat down beside him and said a little impatiently, 'Yes Ballava?'

'Who was that man, Appa?'

'Some visitor from Orissa,' Chinappa looked irritated at being disturbed at his work. 'Said he is travelling around Vijayanagar and wanted to know when this temple will be opened. He wants to watch the pratishthanam ceremonies. I told him the date isn't fixed yet.'

As we walked away, Manjira laughed. 'Nothing suspicious at all.' Ballava joined in. 'Just a visitor, Devayya.'

However, I still wasn't sure that the man was innocent. For an outsider, he spoke very good Kannada. And why come to a temple to discuss anything with Fat Man? I wished I could find out more, but where would I go looking for him in a big city like Vijayanagar?

In the evening at arati time as I helped my father decorate the goddess with flowers, ground the sandalwood and light the tall arati lamp with the nine flames, I kept glancing at the people streaming into the hall. Then the arati began, but the two men did not come. It looked like my little mystery was no mystery at all.

***

At dinner that night as Amma laid the banana leaves before us and served the rice and vegetables, I asked my father, 'Where does the North Road go, Appa?'

Busy eating, he muttered, 'Towards Kampili.'

'Yes, but beyond that? If you went by horse for five days, where would you reach?' I saw Manjira look up and smile at me.

'Why?' Appa looked amused. 'Are you planning to go to Bijapur?'

'Bijapur?' Manjira and I asked, startled. 'But they are our enemies!'

'Yes they are! They have been fighting with Vijayanagar for years,' Appa added and then laughed. 'Now of course our king has really taught them a lesson. Last time they were beaten so badly, the general ran away from the battlefield. Our troops even ransacked the fortress of Gulbarga.'

Bijapur! I thought in confusion. How could anyone from Vijayanagar go to Bijapur when we were still at war? Then Manjira suddenly asked my father, 'And Appa, how do you go to Orissa?'

Appa stopped eating, looked up and stared at us. 'You two are asking too many questions tonight! Planning to travel, are you? Well, Orissa is a long way by boat up the Tungabhadra and Krishna rivers. It would take you weeks.'

Manjira and I decided not to ask any more odd questions that night.

Next morning we were making garlands when a familiar voice called, 'Devayya!' I looked up to see Ballava entering the temple compound. Settling down beside us, he said breathlessly, 'What happened yesterday? Did those suspicious men come again?'

'I thought you didn't believe they were suspicious,' I got back at him for not believing me the day before. And then Manjira and I told him about what we had discovered after talking to Appa.

'Bijapur!' he sounded as startled as we had been. 'How can a man from an enemy kingdom wander around so freely in Vijayanagar?'

'He speaks Kannada and wears clothes like us. I'm pretty sure Fat Man is from here. They meet at the temple with a crowd around them to escape being noticed.'

'But what does he want? Who is he?'

'A spy?' Manjira asked nervously.

'We have to find him,' I said.

It wasn't going to be easy, but we were going to try. Asking our fathers for a day off, we wandered into the heart of the city to begin our search. But at times the sights were so wonderful, we forgot all about looking for Hooked Nose.

We decided to look in the innermost circle of the city where the busy markets were, right before the tall gateway of the Virupaksha Temple. Vijayanagar had rows of walls rising and falling along the many hills like Hemkuta, Malayavanta and Matanga. There were rice fields around the outer walls and many orchards and gardens next to the inner city where noble families lived in beautiful villas. In the heart of the city were the royal palaces, temples and markets, and visitors usually stayed in the houses around these bazaars. I was hoping Hooked Nose had done the same.

Going down the road, Ballava laughed. 'This is fun! I think I'll become a spy catcher instead of a stone carver.'

As we walked down Vijayanagar's main street, I thought no other city could ever have a street as beautiful as this! On both sides were colourful shops selling precious silks, shimmering with brocade or sweet-smelling perfumes. There were crowds at the flower seller's arcade—fragrant with jasmine garlands and piles of roses. At the jewellery shops, noble ladies were looking at gold and silver ornaments set with rubies, diamonds and pearls. And the most delicious smells drifted out of the food shops where they were frying vadas and dosais.

The road was crowded with people wearing elegant clothes as palanquins, carts and horses went past. A nobleman in silks strode towards us with a servant holding a pretty red umbrella over his head. Carts were bringing in goods from distant lands—cotton cloth from Bengal, pepper from Malabar, rice from the land of the Tamils and saffron from the far-off hills of Kashmir.

A bullock cart went past with a beautiful lady sitting in it. Her clothes were of rich silk and even her hair glittered with jewels as her thin silk uttariya flowed in the breeze. 'Oh!' exclaimed Manjira, staring. 'Look! That is Padmalaya, the singer. We heard her on Dussehra last year, remember? I wish I could sing like her.'

That was Manjira's dream. She wanted to be a royal singer, I wanted to carve stones, and Ballava's latest plan was to be a soldier or a spy catcher. We had no idea what fate had in store for us.

Once in a while, remembering our mission, we would ask a passerby or a shopkeeper, 'Do you know where a visitor from Orissa is staying?' We would usually get a puzzled shake of the head in return. Finally, a man who looked like a soldier pointed to a lane and said, 'Look there. Foreign travellers often stay in those guest houses.'

The lane had tall houses on both sides, and at the corner of the entrance, there was a small shop selling paan. Here a plump woman sat folding betel leaves, her own lips red with betel juice. Manjira gave the woman her most winning smile and asked, 'Akka, does a visitor from Orissa stay here?'

'There are people from many lands here,' she replied, while putting pinches of coconut powder on the leaves. 'Some Portuguese have just arrived with horses from the port of Goa. How does this man look?'

'Tall and thin with a hooked ...' Ballava began to

gesture, but I knew a better way to show her. Dipping the tip of a betel leaf in the red paan mix, I drew the man's face on the edge of the brass plate on her counter. The deep-set eyes, the curving nose, the thick lips …

'Oh, that one!' the woman exclaimed. 'See that house with the red steps? He's staying in the room on the ground floor, on the right.'

As we walked away, Ballava gave me a quick look. 'You do draw well, Devayya! You are much better than me. I think you'd make a good sculptor one day.'

'Sure,' I thought, 'that would be the day when the sun rose from the west and the birds flew backwards.'

An old woman was lazily sweeping the steps as we reached the house. 'Amma,' I asked politely, 'is the visitor from Orissa in his room?'

'No. He left a moment ago with his friend.'

'A short fat man?'

'Yes, this man has been here for more than a month but he is hardly ever home. He says he is a trader and has to travel all the time.'

We ran back to the main road looking about us. They could not have gone the way we had come, or we would have spotted them. So we hurried in the opposite direction and suddenly Ballava said, 'There they are!'

Hooked Nose and Fat Man were strolling along just ahead of us and as we dropped behind them, Ballava whispered, 'Don't get too close, Devayya. He might recognise us. Just keep them in sight.'

The road now led to the river and I realised it was getting crowded, with people hurrying in the same direction. I asked a man, 'Where is everyone going, sir?'

'Why, to welcome His Majesty, the king, of course! Didn't you know he is coming back after a tour of the kingdom today? There will be a big procession too.'

At the Talarigattu Ghat, where the ferry crosses the river Tungabhadra, a large crowd was already waiting for the king. We stationed ourselves behind the two men as they squeezed into the crowd and found a spot right next to the river. Across the river I could see the looming brown walls of the Anegundi Fort, and in the river the round boats were busy moving about like ants on a bowl of rice.

'There's the king's ship!' someone shouted, and we all leaned forward to see the tall sails drifting slowly up the river. The bow of the royal ship was shaped like a peacock, the tall mast fluttered with flags and on the deck there were rows of soldiers and sailors holding shiny swords and spears.

As the ship neared the shore, the flutes and drums began to play, the conches began to blow and our king, Maharajadhiraja Krishna Deva Raya, came up on the deck to acknowledge the happy shouts of welcome. Oh, what a majestic sight he made! The tall figure was clad in a golden silk antariya, tied like a dhoti, with an uttariya in deep blue draped over his body. His ears, arms and neck glittered with jewels. He wore a tall cap, bejewelled, like a crown. Followed by his courtiers, he stepped down on the wooden plank bridge and walked towards us.

An elephant swayed on its knees and King Krishna Deva Raya got on the jewelled howdah on top. It was a long procession. First came the drummers and men playing flutes and trumpets, then soldiers in leather jackets on horseback carrying spears that flashed in the sun, followed by elephants and horses carrying the noblemen who surrounded the king. Women stood on the sides throwing flowers and blowing conches. Hooked Nose and Fat Man were watching intently, and suddenly I had an idea. They obviously planned to watch the whole procession, and it would take a while. I could see rows of marching soldiers preparing to follow the king's elephant, and also many chariots. Why didn't we, in the meanwhile, run back and search Hooked Nose's room?

In a flash I had told Ballava and Manjira my plan and we were pushing our way out of the crowd. Then we got lucky and managed to hitch a ride in a bullock cart carrying vegetables to the market. Running hard, we reached the deserted lane, ran up the red steps, turned to the door on the right and then skidded to a stop. There was a big lock hanging on the door.

'There must be windows,' Manjira said.

There was a verandah running in front of the house with a window of the room opening onto it. It was closed too, but as we pushed hard, the wooden shutters slowly screeched open.

Leaving Manjira sitting on the steps as a lookout, Ballava and I climbed into the room and looked around.

It was sparsely furnished—a bed, a small table and an earthen pot of water. There were some clothes in a leather satchel and one pair of shoes. Then, searching quickly, we looked under the mattress and found a small cloth bag. I emptied it out on the bed. There were some copper and silver coins, rolls of linen with writing on them and a knife in a sheath.

We carefully unrolled a sheet of linen each. One had lines and curves drawn in an odd pattern, while on the roll I was holding, there was a row of names and numbers that had been written down in lamp black ink. And then we heard Manjira call from outside. 'Devayya! Oh lord, they are back!'

Ballava snatched the sheets from me and quickly stuffed both of them inside his tunic. Moving as fast as I could, I began stuffing everything back into the cloth bag. By then Ballava had already run across the room and climbed out of the window. As I bent to push the bag under the mattress, I heard the key turn in the lock outside and panicked a bit, realising that the window was too far away. I would never make it outside before the two men came in.

'Run!' I whispered desperately to Ballava and then slid under the bed.

I lay there, trapped, trying to be as still and silent as possible, barely breathing, listening to the door open. Then I heard the men enter and two pairs of feet went past my eyes. Fat Man spoke first. I recognised his slightly whining voice. 'So, my friend, you have finally seen our king.'

'Yes,' said the deep voice of Hooked Nose. 'It does make the job easier. I can spot him quickly in the temple. I cannot make a mistake then ...'

There was the jingle of coins and Fat Man said, 'Thank you! I must be going now. Let us meet at the new temple tonight after midnight and then we can make further plans.'

'Good idea! The place will be deserted and we can move around freely.'

Then, as the feet moved towards the door, Hooked Nose said, 'I'll see you to the road. It is better you do not come to this room again. We can meet at the Pampa Temple at arati time before I leave Vijayanagar.'

'Fine. I'll go there every day.'

Cautiously, I peered out from under the bed and saw the two men walk away and leave the room. In a flash I had crawled out from under the bed and run out of the open door. At the top of the steps I crashed straight into Hooked Nose who was heading back to his room.

'Look where you are going!' he growled, holding me by the arms.

'I'm sorry sir,' I panted. 'I didn't see you.'

The man looked closely at me, still clutching my arms. 'Wait a moment! Haven't I seen you somewhere before?'

My heart began to thud wildly. 'Me?' I opened my eyes wide, trying to look innocent, though my mouth was dry. 'Maybe. I live in the next lane, sir.'

'Hmmm ... He had already lost interest in me as he let me go. 'Maybe.' And walking past, he entered his room and closed the door.

Breathless with relief, I ran as fast as I could down the lane to the corner where Ballava and Manjira waited by the paan shop, their faces creased with anxiety. Quickly walking away, I told them of my adventures and of what I had overheard in the room.

'Seeing the king makes the job easier ...' Manjira mused. 'What could he possibly mean?' Then as we walked silently trying to unravel the significance of the words, Ballava suddenly exclaimed, 'Oh! I nearly forgot about these!' He pulled out the two rolls of linen from under his clothes.

It was afternoon by then and we were feeling very hungry. Settling down under a tree, Manjira opened the bundle of spiced rice we had bought from a shop, and while eating, we studied the sheets of linen.

'Kumara Raya, 10,000,' I read out. 'But that is the name of the king's brother, the Crown Prince!'

'And what do these numbers after each name mean?'

All the while Ballava had been silently studying the second sheet, looking at the strange pattern of lines and curves. 'It's the temple!' he looked up, his eyes wide with shock. 'That's why it looked so familiar to me! It's a crude half complete map of the new temple. See!' His fingers followed the line. 'That's the walled courtyard. This is the temple tank. This is the path from the gateway. The main shrine is marked out, but the rooms inside haven't been drawn.'

'That is why they want to go there tonight!' Manjira exclaimed. 'They want to complete this map. But why?'

I stared at the map as all the words I had overheard in the last three days flashed through my mind, and suddenly everything fell into place. Ballava and Manjira were arriving at the same answer. 'They are planning to kill the king!'

'Hooked Nose was asking about the pratishthanam ceremony ...'

'They'll attack him during the opening ceremony of the new temple!'

We sat there, our heads whirling. Suddenly our "catch a spy" game had become very serious and we did not know what to do.

'We have to warn the king,' Ballava said.

'But that's impossible!' I said. 'Those armed guards at the gate of the palace compound will stop us; we can never reach him. And no one will listen to us anyway.'

Then Manjira said thoughtfully, 'There is Ambika. Maybe she can help.'

'Who?' Ballava frowned.

'Ambika, the devadasi,' I explained. 'She lives in our temple precinct and often dances there. She also dances at the royal court. Queen Tirumale Devi likes her.' And then I looked doubtfully at Manjira. 'Will Ambika believe us?'

'We can try,' she said. Getting up, she added firmly, 'Let's go!'

Ambika the dancer lived in a small house behind our temple. Entering her courtyard, I saw her sitting in her garden threading a jasmine garland for her hair. Looking up, her beautiful lips curved in a smile of welcome. 'Devayya! Manjira! Come in. Are you feeling hungry?'

Ambika loved feeding people.

'No, not today,' I laughed. 'Actually we have come to tell you a long story.'

'How exciting!' she laughed. Ambika was always ready for stories and laughter. 'Tell me, quick!'

So, after introducing Ballava, we began the story of our adventure. Ambika listened silently, her fingers forgetting to thread the flowers, her large eyes fixed intently on our faces. As I finished speaking, she took the linen sheets and studied them. 'These are the names of the king's generals,' she said slowly. 'Prince Kumara Raya is also the commander-in-chief. The numbers must be the soldiers under them.'

'And this,' Ballava pointed out, 'is the map of the new temple.'

'Please help us,' I said desperately. 'The king has to be warned, and you can do that when you dance before him.'

We waited anxiously for Ambika to make up her mind. It took some time. She opened a paan box that lay beside her, stuffed a paan in her mouth, chewed thoughtfully, her face very solemn, and then said, 'Hmmm … Hooked Nose was asking about the pratishthanam ceremony, was he? Do you know what I heard at the palace this morning? The king will announce the date of the temple opening ceremony tomorrow at court.'

'He could ...' Ballava said. 'It can take place the moment the main sanctum is ready. Appa said it is nearly complete.'

'Oh no!' I panicked again. 'If Hooked Nose finds out the date tomorrow, he'll leave for Bijapur immediately. Then how will we catch him?'

'We have to see the king now and he should hear it all from you three,' Ambika said. Then, looking at our doubting faces, she frowned again. 'Hmmm ... now how do I get you three inside? Ah! Of course!' Her eyes shone with excitement. 'Listen, I have a plan for taking you three inside the palace.' That paan had obviously helped her thinking, because her plan was a wonderfully clever one.

A few hours later, as dusk fell over Vijayanagar, Ambika, Manjira, Ballava and I were standing at the gates of the royal harem. This was where the royal women lived, and the king's pleasure palace, the Lotus Mahal, was also here. Manjira was wearing her best clothes, Ballava held a flute, I was carrying a mridangam drum while Ambika walked in front of us holding a basket of flowers.

This was the first time I had been inside the palace area. Ordinary people like us were not allowed inside. I looked around and thought Lotus Mahal was such a delightful palace. The two-storied building had domes and arched doorways now bright with lamps. As the female guards let us in, one of them said, 'You are dancing again tonight, Ambi?' Ambika just gave her a mysterious smile.

The guard led us down a corridor to the royal chamber and for a moment I stood still, looking around at the magnificent decorations. The tall pillars were carved and covered with an inlay of silver patterns, and on the floor were gorgeous rugs. The room smelled of incense and flowers. Ambika had told us that this was His Majesty King Krishna Deva Raya's resting chamber, where every evening he watched dancers, heard singers and poets reciting their newest creations.

As we stood at the door waiting to enter, I noticed that at the far end of the room on a raised platform there was a cushioned throne and the king sat on it, leaning on silk bolsters. A beautiful lady wearing silks and a lot of jewellery sat next to him.

'Who are all these people,' I asked in a whisper, 'with the king?'

'The lady is Her Majesty Queen Tirumale Devi,' Ambika whispered back. 'And that man sitting on a cushion on the step below is Tenali Raman, the poet and wit.' And I looked again at the dark smiling face of the man whose jokes were repeated all across Vijayanagar.

As we bowed before him, the king smiled. 'Ah! Ambika! What a pleasant surprise. What are you dancing tonight?'

'Your Highness!' Ambika gave a naughty smile. 'Tonight I'm not going to dance for you.'

'Oh!' Queen Tirumale Devi looked startled. 'I did not know you had other talents, Ambi!'

'If Your Highness would permit, I would like this little girl to sing to you.' And Ambika pushed forward a shy Manjira as I looked nervously at the king. Suppose he said that he was not interested in listening to little girls? But Krishna Deva Raya was in a good mood and he waved benignly. 'Begin!'

Manjira sang one of her favourite songs based on Raga Jaimangala in Adi Talam about peacocks dancing in the rainy season. Her voice shook a bit in the beginning and then she gained confidence and began to sing beautifully. I felt so proud of my little sister. Fortunately she sang so well that the king did not notice that Ballava and I were not playing the musical instruments we were holding. It would have been a disaster if I had to play the mridangam!

Finishing her song, Manjira bowed and Krishna Deva Raya smiled. 'Yes. She is worth listening to, Ambika.' The Queen and Tenali Raman were also smiling at her. Then Ambika put the basket of flowers in Manjira's hand and pushed her forward. On top of the flowers were the two rolls of linen. Bowing low, Manjira held the flowers up for Krishna Deva Raya who leaned forward. Then his hand stilled as he saw the rolls of linen. He picked them up and frowned. 'What is this, Ambika? You know I don't listen to requests in the inner mahal.'

'Please, Your Highness,' Ambika pleaded, 'these are not requests. If you will just take a look …'

Krishna Deva Raya unrolled the sheets and then studied them. He looked puzzled by the map, but when he began reading the list of names, his face became still with attention. 'Where did you get this, Ambi? Who gave this to you? This is treason!' and the anger in his deep voice made my heart quake.

But from somewhere I found the courage to look up at him and say, 'We found them, Your Highness.'

Haltingly, our voices cracking with nervousness, somehow, between the three of us, we told His Majesty everything we knew about Hooked Nose and Fat Man. In the beginning his face was full of disbelief but slowly the frown changed to close attention. His eyes never left our faces and I began to feel he believed us. Tenali Raman also sat leaning forward, listening intently to our words.

As we finished our tale, the king turned to Tenali Raman and asked, 'What do you think? What are they planning to do?'

Tenali Raman studied the linen sheets, looked up and said, 'The North Road only leads to Bijapur. It looks like Bijapur is planning to invade Vijayanagar on the day of the temple opening. Their spies will attack you inside the temple while you are at worship and not too heavily guarded. Many of the generals will also be there in the temple when the Bijapur army attacks our borders. It is a very clever plan.'

'And I will be at worship and not carrying any weapons,' Krishna Deva Raya said. Then he turned to us and said, 'Take soldiers to that house and catch that spy …' He paused and asked me, 'What did you call him?'

'Hooked Nose,' Tenali Raman said with a smile.

'But Your Majesty, by now they could be at the temple site,' I said. 'They planned to meet there at midnight.'

'And Your Majesty,' Ballava added quickly, 'I know the area well. My father and I work there. He is the Chief

Sculptor, Chinappa. I can take the soldiers through the back entrance.'

'Go!' Krishna Deva Raya waved his hand.

'May Lord Krishna be with you,' Queen Tirumale Devi added as Tenali Raman hurried out to call the soldiers.

Half an hour later Ballava and I were leading a band of ten soldiers up the hill towards the new temple. Ambika and Manjira had headed home. Far away I could see the light of the beacon fire lit on Hemkuta Hill that guides travellers to Vijayanagar and tells our enemies that Vijayanagar is always awake.

Finally we were at the top of the steep slope of boulders, right behind the main temple building, and peered past the wall. The place looked deserted with just patches of moonlight and shadows. It was all still and silent till a bird screeched somewhere. It was past midnight, but the two men had not arrived. We squatted in the shadow of the temple and waited, looking down the slope of the hill.

My eyes had become used to the dark, and I could see very clearly, and as I caught the first faint movement down the slope, I whispered to the others, 'Here they come!' The two familiar shadows, one tall, one short, moved closer.

Then I heard Fat Man say, 'You better finish checking out the site tonight. Then you can take the drawings with you tomorrow.'

'I have to see the inner rooms,' Hooked Nose said. 'Those stone carvers did not allow me inside that morning.

I have to know where the king will sit. Then once I know the date of the opening, I'll leave immediately.'

By then they were at the door of the temple when the leader of the soldiers said firmly, 'Now!' In a flash, the soldiers had jumped out and landed around the two men. But they were not going to give up without a fight. The two men pulled out their swords and I could hear the clang of clashing metal as Hooked Nose and Fat Man fought desperately to hold back the soldiers. Then a soldier swung his arm in a quick arc and Fat Man's sword slipped out of his hand. Immediately he was surrounded by the soldiers.

Realising that everyone was busy with Fat Man, Hooked Nose turned suddenly and began to run up the slope, but he did not realise that Ballava and I were in his way. We sprang forward and dived at him and caught his ankles. He went crashing to the ground with an angry yell, and in a moment the soldiers had

surrounded him and tied him up. The king had wanted the men to be caught alive.

As we stood there watching the soldiers lead the two men away, it suddenly hit me that we had caught the spy from Bijapur. The three of us and Ambika had saved Vijayanagar from war.

After questioning Hooked Nose, the complete plot was revealed. He gave Fat Man away. He had maps of the fortification walls of Vijayanagar. He had planned to kill the king. Fat Man was the traitor from our city. Our king rewarded us with money, of course, but the Queen's gifts made us much happier. At her orders, Manjira was to begin lessons with the great singer Padmalaya. Ballava was offered a soldier's training but then he thought it over and decided he would stay a stone carver after all.

And as for me, Tenali Raman came and spoke to my father. Then, on an auspicious morning, I sat down beside Ballava and his father Chinappa as they showed me the right way to hold a chisel over a piece of granite stone and hit it with a hammer.

I, Devayya, a priest's son, was going to become a sculptor.

A month later we were in the front row watching Maharajadhiraja Krishna Deva Raya begin the worship at the new Krishna temple. Ballava's father and my guru Chinappa the head sculptor stood proudly on one side as the king did the puja that was being directed by my father. The bells clanged, conches blew and a hundred Brahmin priests chanted mantras as the king poured ghee into the sacred fire. Later, as Padmalaya sang, Ambika danced for us.

....

HISTORICAL NOTE

Vijayanagar was the most powerful empire of south India from the 14th to the 16th century and Krishna Deva Raya was its greatest king. The kingdom was surrounded by enemies like Bijapur, Golconda and Orissa and Krishna Deva Raya defeated them all. His kingdom included most of modern Andhra Pradesh, Karnataka and Tamil Nadu. The ruins of his Krishna temple still stand near the Virupaksha temple at Hampi.

The city of Vijyanagar was the richest in the land with traders from many countries coming there. Among them were Arabs, Chinese, Persians, Portuguese and Italians, and many of them wrote their memoirs from where we get a portrait of a magnificent city filled with bazaars, temples, palaces and a people who enjoyed music, dance and literature.

Vijayanagar was a generous, tolerant city where people of every race and religion were welcome. It was also quite relaxed about caste, and people could choose any profession they wanted. The famous Narasimha statue that is like a symbol of Vijayanagar was in fact carved by a Brahmin named Krishnabhatta.

In 1565 AD a combined army of Vijayanagar's enemies attacked and defeated the kingdom. They looted, burned and destroyed the city and people fled, never to return. The ruins of Vijayanagar can be seen at Hampi in Karnataka.

....

MAKING STONES DANCE

For me the sound is as beautiful as music—the soft tap tap tappity tap of a hammer gently hitting a chisel and the chink chink of the chisel cutting into stone. I sometimes hear it in my dreams. My friend Bhaskara laughs when I say that newly cut stone has a smell—a sharp, clear and mellow aroma like a fresh breeze.

One morning I was working next to my father, and as always I was spending more time watching him than carving stone. He was working slowly and carefully on a necklace worn by Lord Vishnu, the chips of stone flying around him. He was carving the pattern of precious stones in a flower setting and I sat wondering in amazement at how his chisel could lightly chip off a little stone and in the next tap cut deep in a neat curve. I still don't know how he can make the chisel carve as if he is cutting through a soft lump of butter and not a stubborn hard chunk of granite or marble.

As you must have guessed by now, my father Ramanatha is a carver of stone and I am his son Keshava. One day I want to be a chief shilpin like him—the chief sculptor working at the site for a temple or a palace. He is one of the best sculptors in the kingdom of Vijayanagar and is the head of the team of stone carvers who are working on the Vishnu temple being built in the city. He supervises the other carvers in the sculptor's yard who are working on pillars, walls and ceiling panels, and draws all the designs.

The men were at work all around us, bent over pieces of stone. The air was filled with stone dust and the sound of hammers hitting chisels. Appa was busy carving the image of Lord Vishnu and he was working in a separate sculptor's shed. One day this idol will stand in the sanctum of the temple and will be worshipped with flowers and incense, offered fruits and sweets, but right now it is just a rough piece of black marble on which the figure of Vishnu is slowly emerging as if rising out of water. The shape of his body is clear, his clothes and jewellery are half done but the god's face is still a blank oval. Appa always carves the face at the end.

'Appa, when will you carve Vishnu's crown?' I asked as he blew at the stone to clear away the stone dust.

'After I finish the jewellery. Aren't you supposed to do a border on that pillar? Get to work, Keshava!' With a sigh I went back to the pillar. Appa always sounds impatient when I ask him anything, but how will I learn if I can't ask questions?

'Oye Keshava! You're still making those bells on the pillar?' asked an amused voice from above me.

Looking up, squinting against the sun, I saw Bhaskara's grinning face.

'You really work fast, don't you? The pillar looks exactly the same as it did yesterday!'

As he sat down by my side, I asked, 'How did you get away so early? Have the king's elephants run away?'

'Not a chance! I just sneaked off when Appa wasn't looking.'

Bhaskara's father takes care of the king's elephants and Bhaskara also has to work at the elephant stables. The elephants are kept in a row of open rooms near the zenana palaces, and, as Bhaskara says, the animals live in more comfort than we do. Their stables are a long row of granite rooms that look like a palace with pillars and a domed roof. Every day the floor is covered with clean straw and they are given fresh leaves, grass and fruits and vegetables to eat.

Once, while feeding bananas to an elephant, Bhaskara had sighed, 'In my next birth I want to be an elephant in the royal stables.'

Bhaskara does not like working in the stables. He thinks carving stones is so much more fun. He spends all his free time beside me in the sculptor's yard and I am teaching him to carve. He has learnt a lot in the last few months and would love it if Appa would teach him. But we haven't had the courage to ask him. At least he hasn't said anything about Bhaskara working on the pillar.

So I pulled out a spare set of hammer and chisel from my bag and Bhaskara got to work. Appa wanted a row of bells hanging from long chains and a curving pattern of flowers and vines as the border. In the middle there was to be a carving of the goddess Lakshmi by a senior sculptor. I am still not allowed to carve the figures. I was doing the bells, and Bhaskara was tapping away at the flowers. We were concentrating hard as you have to tap carefully and keep screwing up your eyes, because sometimes chips of stone come flying and hit your face.

The sudden loud voice above us made us jump. 'Ramanatha Swamy! What is this boy doing here?'

I looked up and saw the white dhoti-clad figure of Rajendran glaring down at us. We stood up and did namaskar. After all, he was an important man, the supervising priest at the temple site. Whenever you build a temple, you need a priest who tells you the direction the temple should face and where the sanctum has to be built. He chooses the images of the deities that are carved on the walls and pillars. Of course, Rajendran only orders people about; he never does any of the real work. That is left to the carvers, masons and bricklayers.

'I am Keshava, sir, son of the shilpin Ramanatha Swamy, and this is my friend Bhaskara.'

'I am just helping Keshava with the pillar,' Bhaskara added politely.

By then Appa had come up to see what was happening. He looked the priest straight in the eye and said, 'You have a problem, you come to me. Don't shout at the boys.'

'Of course I have a problem!' He waved a disdainful hand at Bhaskara. 'We can't have a stable boy carving a temple pillar. He is of low caste and therefore unclean. He will ruin everything!'

'This is not a pillar for the temple sanctum. I'm teaching the boys to carve, and if the pillar is good enough to be used, it will be placed in one of the outer halls. These boys are just fourteen and they are learning the craft. They do not know enough carving to work on the main temple.'

'But he belongs to a low caste. He is a stable boy!'

'He's my student and I have allowed him to work with Keshava. If you have a problem, why don't you complain to Ranga Nayaka? He will be coming to inspect the work this afternoon.'

With an angry glare Rajendran stalked off as Bhaskara looked nervously at Appa. 'Sir, should I go away? I don't want any trouble ...'

Appa smiled and pointed at a man across the yard who was busy carving. 'See that man? His father worked with leather because he comes from a lower caste than yours. His work is so good, he is carving panels for the temple ceiling.'

'Does Rajendran know?'

'Of course not! But Ranga Nayaka does.'

As Appa turned to go, Bhaskara skipped behind him, stammering with nervousness. 'Th… then sir … what you said … Am I your student then?'

'Maybe …' and Appa walked off.

When we went back to working on the pillar, I could hear Bhaskara humming happily as he carefully carved the petal of a flower.

That afternoon, Ranga Nayaka came to inspect our work. He was one of the most powerful noblemen in Vijayanagar, a famous general who had won many battles. He was building this temple to celebrate his victory over the army of Golconda that had attacked a border fortress he was guarding.

I saw Ranga Nayaka step out of his palanquin and enter the sculptor's yard. The nobleman was a tall man with the broad shoulders and narrow waist of a warrior, though of course today he carried no weapons. He wore a simple cotton angavastram and a short tunic, his long hair knotted at the nape of his neck. He wore gold bangles and many rings.

Then I saw the plump figure of Rajendran go running up to him, bowing like a puppet, as with a wide smile he called out, 'Welcome, Your Honour! Welcome!'

'Our Rajendran is like a snake, isn't he?' I muttered.

Appa walked beside Ranga Nayaka as he went from carver to carver to see what they were doing. Rajendran walked beside them trying to put forth his own opinion about the carving, though he knew nothing about it. I thought Appa was being very patient letting him chatter on like that. As they came towards us, I saw Rajendran point at Bhaskara and whisper something into Ranga Nayaka's ear, and the general nodded. His face was expressionless.

'So you are Ramanatha's son? Let's see what you have done.' And Ranga Nayaka was taking a close look at the pillar. Then he turned to Bhaskara and asked, 'Are you carving these flowers?' Bhaskara nodded. 'Well, they look prettier than your friend's bells!' he said. He and Appa laughed. 'Well, Ramanatha, it looks like we have two good carvers here! They will carry the tradition forward.'

'Thank you sir but I am actually a stable hand's son,' Bhaskara said a little nervously. 'My father works in the royal elephant's stables.'

'I know.' The general's eyes were kind. He pointed to one of the soldiers standing beside his palanquin. 'See that man? He is my best sword fighter and has saved my life many times on the battlefield. His father is a weaver, his name is Rafiq and he is a Muslim. I trust him with my life.'

As Ranga Nayaka walked away, I looked around. Rajendran had vanished and Bhaskara was grinning so widely I could see all his teeth gleaming in the sun.

'Get back to work!' said Appa, striding off.

Six months later most of the temple was ready and so was the image of Lord Vishnu. It now stood ready to be placed in the sanctum of the temple. Appa had carved Vishnu as Vaikuntha Perumal, the Lord of the Universe. So he looked like a celestial king, wearing a lot of jewellery

and a tall crown. In his four hands he carried the chakra, the conch shell, a mace and a lotus flower. Once the idol was placed in the sanctum, he would of course be covered with real gold jewellery, wear silk garments and lots of flower garlands.

One evening after everyone had left we went into the sculptor's shed and found Appa sitting before the image of Vishnu. He had lit a small earthen lamp and put a handful of rose petals and jasmines at the god's feet. He was praying silently. We sat down beside him quietly.

I looked at Lord Vaikuntha Perumal's dark, calm, smiling face. It seemed to be alive as it moved in and out of the light and shadow in the flickering light of the lamp. Appa always did this small puja alone after he completed an idol. It was his way of saying thank you to the god. I looked up at the shadowed eyes and the calm smiling lips and wondered amazed at how Appa could give life to a piece of stone. When he carves a beautiful goddess he can make the stone smile, and when he creates the image of Nataraja, the dancing image of Lord Shiva, it is as if the stone begins to dance.

Appa put a dot of sandalwood paste on Vishnu's forehead and said quietly, as if speaking to the god, 'I will not be able to worship you again, my Lord Vaikuntha Perumal, so please accept my prayers now.'

Bhaskara sat up, his eyes wide with surprise. 'Why? Why can't you worship the god again?'

'Because, in a few days, during the pratisthanam

ceremony, Vaikuntha Perumal will be placed in the sanctum of the temple and I cannot go inside.'

'How can that be?' Bhaskara looked shocked. 'You carved the idol!'

'I know. But I'm just a carver of stone.' Leaving the lamp burning before the idol, we came out of the shed. 'Once he is the deity in a temple only the high caste priests, royalty and noblemen are allowed inside. Not a low caste person like me.' We were now walking out of the temple precinct. 'If I want to do puja I'll have to stand at the door and the priest will carry my offerings of flowers inside. I can't put a garland around the god or sandalwood on his feet. I can no longer touch him.'

'But Appa, for months you were the only one who touched him!' I was feeling very, very angry.

'It is so unfair!' Bhaskara protested.

Appa laughed, 'What can I do? That is the way it is.' By then we were going past the Vitthala temple that stood at the end of the road and he reached out and lovingly touched one of the gateways. 'I carved this too when I was young. Who remembers? Everyone calls it King Krishna Deva Raya's temple. No one remembers the names of the shilpin who created it.'

'Even I didn't know!' I said regretfully.

'That is because no one says this is Kartikeyan's temple. He was the sculptor who planned the temple, designed those beautiful pillars, carved the stone chariot and the images around the sanctum.' There was such a deep sadness in his voice that it made me forget to breathe. 'No one remembers Kartikeyan, and like him, very soon I will be forgotten too.'

A few days later the pratisthanam ceremony took place at the Vishnu temple. All the shilpin and their families stood in the outer hall watching the queens, princes, princesses, noblemen and their families arrive in palanquins. Everyone was dressed in their best silk clothes and wearing a lot of jewellery. The women had adorned their hair with flowers. The guests stood in the inner hall right before the sanctum where they could see the ceremony while we could only catch a glimpse of it by craning our necks.

Inside the sanctum Lord Vaikuntha Perumal stood glittering in jewels, wearing a golden silk dhoti. A red silk scarf was wrapped over his body. Diamonds and gold jewellery gleamed on his neck and arms and he wore a tall gold crown. Rows of brass lamps made the sanctum glow in a mellow golden light and the air was filled with the fragrance of incense. I peered past a pillar to look at the god Appa had created. I thought Lord Vishnu had looked kinder and more like a true god, handsome and kind, standing in the thatched sculptor's shed with just a single earthen lamp to light his face and a handful of rose petals at his feet.

Then King Krishna Deva Raya arrived, escorted by Ranga Nayaka and accompanied by his two queens. I had seen the king before, but never this close. Our king now had grey hair but his tall figure was slim as before and as always, he was dressed simply in white silk. He had an interesting face, with high cheekbones and large deep-set eyes. One day I would like to carve such a face because it is both strong and kind and he always smiles at people. Now he came up to us and spoke to Appa and the other stone carvers, praising the temple. He also gave the men new clothes and money, and Appa got a bag of gold coins for having carved the lord's image.

Just as the king entered the sanctum, the bells rang, the conches blew and the priests began to recite the Sanskrit mantras. As the puja began, in the outer hall the two temple dancers, the devadasis Madhavi and Pallavi, began to dance to welcome the god into the temple, swaying and turning among the pillars like two gorgeous butterflies.

Watching the devadasis, I thought they were temple dancers who were supposed to be married to the god of the temple. That is what the word devadasi means—handmaiden to the god. But even they were not allowed to enter the sanctum, and like Appa, they too had to stand outside. I knew the two women. They were true devotees of Vishnu and were also very well educated. They sang the songs they had composed, and danced on them too. They probably knew better Sanskrit than that fat priest Rajendran but just because he was born a brahmin, Rajendran, who had done nothing to build this temple, would now sit in the sanctum and worship Vishnu every day.

Next morning I shared my thoughts with Bhaskara as we were sitting beside the Tungabhadra river, watching the water sparkle and shimmer in the early morning light.

'Even though he is a bad-tempered fool, Rajendran is supposed to be a better man than our fathers and the devadasis just because he is a brahmin?' I argued. 'What kind of justice is that? Shouldn't the gods judge us by our actions and not by our birth?'

'What will you do?' Bhaskara zipped a stone across the water, making it skip and skim. 'Cut off his pigtail?'

I grinned. 'Not a bad idea! He snores away on the back verandah every afternoon, so it would be easy. But that is not good enough. I want Appa to be remembered as the sculptor of the Vishnu idol.' I just could not forget the sadness in his voice as he said, 'I'll be forgotten.'

Bhaskara turned and stared at me, puzzled. 'How?'

'By carving it on the idol. I want to carve Appa's name on the image of Vishnu. So people will always know the name of the sculptor.'

Bhaskara was silent for a long while and then said, 'How will we get into the sanctum? It's always locked, and Rajendran has the keys.'

I remembered that a big padlock hung on the door when Rajendran was away and he had the key and its duplicate hanging on a thread that he tied to his waist and tucked into his dhoti.

Both of us thought hard for a while. 'We have to steal one key. There are two of them,' I said finally.

'He'll notice one key is missing.'

'Not if we put another key in its place.'

Bhaskara looked admiringly at me. 'Keshava, my

friend! You will make a great burglar! And I'll make a great burglar's assistant because I know exactly how we can steal the key!'

Next morning we were at the river bank before the sun had come out, and sat waiting behind a tree. We knew that soon Rajendran would come for his bath and he'd be there at sunrise to say his prayers. In the dim dawn light we saw him walk towards the river, yawning as he went down the stone steps of the ghat. He left his bundle of fresh clothes on the ghat steps and waded into the river. We crept closer and then as the first rays of the sun turned the eastern sky a soft pink, Rajendran picked up a handful of water, closed his eyes and began to loudly recite the Gayatri mantra in praise of the rising sun.

Within seconds we had streaked down the steps to the pile of clothes, pulled out one key, put in another and were back behind the tree by the time he had finished his prayers. After his bath, he came up, put on his clothes, casually tied the thread with the keys around his waist and walked away.

I looked at the key in my hand. 'Tonight!'

That evening there was quite a crowd at the temple for the evening aarti ceremony. Rajendran worshipped Vaikuntha Perumal with a tall brass lamp glittering with twenty one flames. Then we got a sprinkling of holy water and a small sweet as prasad. Everyone went home after that except Bhaskara and me. We went and hid in a dark corner in the outer hall and waited for the temple to become empty. I was carrying my hammer and chisel in a bag.

Rajendran came out of the sanctum, clanged the door shut, shot the bolt and then pulled out his keys. As we held our breath, he shoved a key into the lock and the key got stuck.

'Oh Lord Vishnu, help!' I prayed. 'He's used the wrong key!'

Rajendran pulled out the key and looked at it with a frown and then used the other one. It turned smoothly and the lock clicked home. He gave a puzzled shake of his head and walked away.

'Oh, thank god he's such an idiot!' Keshava whispered in relief. Then we followed at a distance up to the gate to make sure he left the temple.

In a flash we had opened the door and slid into the sanctum and closed the door behind us. I felt my heart thud as I looked at Lord Vishnu. He stood with a small lamp burning before him. We went behind the image and I took out my hammer and chisel. I knew what I wanted to carve, and exactly where.

Appa had carved a lovely border of half open lotus buds and curving lotus leaves all around the base of the image. I placed each word carefully in the middle of the flowers and they merged so neatly into the design that the words would not be easy to spot. Tapping softly, making sure they were not easily visible against the black marble, I carved the words, 'This image was carved by the shilpin Ramanatha Swamy of Vijayanagar.'

It was past midnight when we came out of the temple. My heart was still thudding madly and I was covered in sweat. The roads were silent as we hurried home. Bhaskara and I were grinning at each other in relief as we took huge gulps of air. Then we realised what we had done and we jumped and hugged each other. We couldn't stop laughing.

Who cares what the brahmin priests say about high and low castes or high and low births? My low caste friend Bhaskara had been inside the sanctum and no disaster had taken place. We had both touched the image of Lord Vishnu and the god had only smiled kindly at us. Lord Vishnu did not judge us by our birth; people like Rajendran did. And we do not have to obey other people.

Now the name of my low caste Appa, son of a stone carver, guru of a stable hand, will always be there with Lord Vaikuntha Perumal. As long as the temple stood, the world would never ever forget him.

We had made sure of that.

....

HISTORICAL NOTE

Vijayanagar was the most powerful empire of South India between the 14th and 16th centuries. Its greatest ruler was the warrior-poet King Krishna Deva Raya and his kingdom included most of the

Deccan peninsula. Even though the kings were devout Hindus, Vijayanagar was a very liberal empire where people of every religion were allowed to live in peace. Muslims were employed in the army and allowed to build mosques, and Jains built temples and ran businesses. Women lived freely. Many were employed as officers in the government and some were even wrestlers. The capital city of Vijayanagar was the richest city in India and traders from far-off places like China, Malaya, Portugal and Russia wandered around its fabulous bazaars, amazed at the prosperity of the people. Today you can see the ruins of Vijayanagar at Hampi, Karnataka.

....

MAKING A PEACOCK SMILE

This time it was a dancing peacock.

It was drawn with sharp, confident lines on the outer walls of the haveli garden with a piece of brick. The peacock was dancing with its tail fanning out behind it, and what caught his eye was that the reddish coloured bird had a small, flirtatious smile on his beaky face.

Mir Sayyid Ali laughed.

For the last one week he had been spotting these tantalising drawings along the road he took to his studio, an array of birds, animals, trees, flowers and faces waiting for him at sudden corners. They were drawn on stray patches of walls, large boulders, the half-built pillar of a palace and on a tree trunk. Once a cat face had peered out from behind a gateman's hut and grinned at him. They were all drawn using broken pieces of brick. He could see the pieces lying on the ground, but the artist was never around.

Mir Sayyid Ali was used to people trying to get his attention. After all, he was a famous man. Everyone in the kingdom of Badshah Akbar knew that he was the head of the tasveer khana, the famous studio of miniature painters. Many young artists tried to become his students. They came to his studio carrying bundles of sketches and begged to be allowed the honour of becoming his student or shagird. Some offered him money while others were willing to be his servant without pay. They all knew that he was a choosy man and took on very few apprentices.

However, in all these years, no one had drawn peacocks on his garden wall to get his attention, and as he studied the sketch with a critical eye, he had to admit that it was drawn very well. He really liked the detailed depiction of the tail, the long eyelashes and that curving bird smile.

'When will this boy come out of hiding?' he wondered as he walked past the gateway that led to the dargah of Sheikh Salim Chishti and stopped to bow his head and say a quick prayer to his favourite Sufi saint. 'Sheikh Sahib,' he thought, 'who are you sending to my doorstep now?'

Then, wrapping his woollen shawl around himself, Mir Sayyid Ali walked on, past the high-walled palaces of Fatehpur Sikri. Akbar's new city was still being built, the red sandstone palaces where the royal family lived were already occupied, but the havelis of the courtiers were still coming up along the slope of the hill. There was a change of guards at the gateway with one group of soldiers marching off and another marching in with a lot of thumping of boots, clanging of swords and shouting of orders.

It was very early. Sayyid Ali loved this time of the day as Fatehpur Sikri woke up all around him. The winter sun was still a soft, smudgy glow behind the swirling mist, and there were few people around except for the servants and maids heading to work. The cleaning women were raising a cloud of dust as they swept away the leaves that had fallen on the cobbled pathways.

Then he was at the door of the karkhana, the painters' studio. It was a big airy pillared pavillion where the miniature painters worked. As always he was the first to arrive and the karkhana assistant Bulaki was still sweeping the floor, making a pile of strips of paper, bits of charcoal, broken paint jars and chewed up brushes.

'A peacock today,' Sayyid Ali said, taking off his shawl, 'this time right on my garden wall. And the peacock had long eyelashes and smiled.'

Bulaki laughed. 'He's getting closer. One day he'll stand in your baithak and scratch on the floor.'

'I wish he would; then at least I would be able to meet him.'

The whole karkhana knew of the mysterious artist drawing his portfolio on the walls of Fatehpur Sikri to entice Sayyid Ali. So, later in the day, as the painters sat in patches of sunlight before their wooden tables, they talked as they worked. They were all bent over rectangles of handmade paper, with bundles of brushes and paints that were mixed in large clam shells beside them. Many kinds of painting were slowly emerging under their hands—the king on his elephant leading his army, a dancing girl with her skirt flaring around her as she whirled, a herd of deer in a forest or the siege of a fortress, all drawn in fine delicate lines and coloured in bejewelled hues.

'Can he draw?' Mukund asked as he mixed a deep emerald paint in a clam shell. 'Show any talent?'

Sayyid Ali, bent over a painting, carefully drawing the outlines of grey clouds, grunted, 'Yes.'

'You leave your house an hour after dawn and this boy completes his drawing even before that?' Basawan looked up, holding a brush. 'When does he do it? He can't draw at night.'

'Today I had a feeling he was watching me from somewhere. I'm going to get up early and catch him tomorrow,' Sayyid Ali muttered with an irritated shake of his head. 'I think he'll draw on the other side of the garden wall next, and I'll be there.'

Just then his old friend Khwaja Abdus Samad walked into the studio and heard him. 'Planning to kidnap an artist, eh Sayyid? I've never heard of that before. He must be worth the trouble ...'

'He is. He made a peacock smile.'

***

The boy was lost in his drawing and did not hear Sayyid Ali when he walked up in his slippers to stand behind him. It was so early, the sun was still hidden behind the mist, and the light was a grey metallic gloom. It was barely light enough to see, and here he was, drawing away.

This time he was sketching a caparisoned elephant, and Sayyid Ali noticed in surprise that he did not start by drawing the body of the animal. Instead, he began at one end, with the trunk, and then with sure, quick lines there was the head, the ears and the body. Then he was moving down to add the legs and feet. It looked like the elephant was in motion.

'It's as if the whole picture is there, clear as daylight, in his head,' Sayyid Ali thought, 'and his hand just follows his imagination.'

As the boy now began to add a cloth covering on the back of the elephant and then a howdah on top, he took a closer look at the young absorbed face. The boy was about fourteen, tall and thin, wearing a full-sleeved quilted cotton jacket over his kurta pyjamas, the narrow dusty feet thrust into battered old chappals. His face looked unwashed and his long hair was tousled and uncombed as if he had come straight from bed. As the piece of brick he was using crumbled and broke in his fingers, he looked at his left palm where he held more pieces.

'The trunk is usually longer,' Sayyid Ali said quietly, 'and the ears are a bit smaller.'

The boy whipped around, his eyes widening in panic as the pieces of brick fell from his hand. He turned as if to

flee, but Sayyid Ali stepped forward and held his arm in a tight grip.

'I want to talk to you.'

'Huzoor ... I'm sorry ... are you angry with me?' the boy mumbled in the cracked voice of a teenager. 'I just ...'

'I'm not angry at all. I just want to talk to you. What's your name, son?'

'Surjan Singh.' Noticing that Sayyid Ali was smiling, the boy's face flooded with relief. Sayyid Ali put his arm around his narrow shoulders.

'Shall we go inside? This cold is not good for my old bones, Surjan. Now I need some hot milk.' He frowned at the young face. 'Must you draw so early in the day?'

And suddenly, to his surprise, Surjan was dipping down and touching his feet.

Inside, the boy and the old man sat by a small coal chulah with bowls of milk flavoured with saffron. Sayyid Ali looked kindly at the high-cheekboned, large-eyed young face. The boy had not spoken after they had come inside. 'So, Surjan, tell me about your life. Where do you stay?'

With a quick flick of the head, he said, 'In the soldiers' quarters behind the palaces ...' and then fell silent again.

'Your father is a soldier then?'

Another silent nod. It looked like Sayyid Ali was going to have a tough time making the boy talk.

'Where is he stationed?'

'My father came here with the princess' escort from Amber when she came to marry the Badshah.'

'Oh, so you are a Rajput?'

'Ji, we came from Amber, Raja Man Singh's kingdom in the desert. I was quite small when we came here. I don't remember it much.'

'And now you want to become a painter, hmm?'

'Can I … I mean … become a painter …'

'Maybe. You have talent, but that's just the beginning. You'll have to work very hard for many years while you are being trained at the karkhana.'

The young face bloomed with joy, the thin cheeks flushing. 'You liked what I was drawing, huzoor?'

'Some of them, but you have much to learn. It takes years to become a mussawir.'

'A what?'

'We painters are called mussawirs. In the beginning you'll be an apprentice under another painter and you will help all the artists in the studio.'

'I'll do anything you want, huzoor, work at the karkhana or in your house, clean, cook … but I don't have any money for fees …'

'Did I ask you for any?' Sayyid Ali's grey eyebrows rose. 'In Badshah Akbar's karkhanas, all the apprentices are paid a salary while they learn.'

'A salary? *Sach*?' Surjan's eyes were blazing with excitement. 'And I was willing to work just for food!'

Sayyid Ali was enjoying the many expressions flickering across the young face. 'First we have to get your father's permission, of course.'

Suddenly the light went out of the boy's eyes. 'Do we have to?'

'Why? Will he refuse?'

'I know he will. He wants me to be a soldier like him and he hates it when I draw. I had done some paintings on the walls of our house and he covered them with whitewash saying they were ugly, and he threw away my brushes. He says that a Rajput does not play with colours and brushes; it is unmanly.'

'What will he do if you tell him you are joining the karkhana?'

'Beat me again.' Surjan's expressive face had become still, his eyes remembering the pain. 'He beats us all, huzoor ... my mother, my sister, me. Whenever he drinks at night, he comes looking for us.'

Sayyid Ali sat silent for a while and then said, 'Then we don't need his permission. I am giving you a job. And don't worry; he won't have the courage to beat me, and if he tried, the Badshah will have him whipped. You can stay at the karkhana and help my assistant Bulaki.'

The large eyes were still shadowed with fear. 'He'll come looking for me.'

'It won't be easy to find you. The karkhana is at the other end of Sikri, below the hill. There are many other studios and workshops there and only the people who work there know the place.'

The boy stood up. 'Let's go then!' he said happily.

'Patience, son,' the old man got up slowly. 'I had to get up very early so I could catch you. Now I need a massage and a warm bath and … he glanced at Surjan's old, grimy clothes, the torn chappals and smudged face. 'You need a bath too. I think my son's old clothes will fit you.'

'I can give you a massage, huzoor …' the boy raised his palms and waved his fingers. 'I have good hands.'

'That was the idea.'

An hour later, Mir Sayyid Ali, now warmly clad in wool, walked towards the karkhana with Surjan, looking clean and well-dressed, skipping impatiently beside him. Suddenly the boy had found his voice.

'The karkhana must be a wonderful place, janaab, with so many painters!'

'I'm not your huzoor or janaab … call me Ustad. I'm your teacher now.'

A huge sigh of joy. 'Ji Ustad!'

At the karkhana, Bulaki came hurrying out. 'Caught him, Ustad?'

'Caught him. Meet Surjan Singh, our new apprentice. You've been asking for an assistant, so here he is. He'll do the washing, cleaning and shopping in the morning and then help the artists in the studio. He'll also stay here. I think I'll get Basawan to teach him.'

Surjan had not only found his voice but also got his spirit back. He bent and touched a surprised Bulaki's feet. 'I'll be your slave, Bulaki dada.'

'He also touches feet at the slightest excuse,' Sayyid Ali grinned at Surjan's happy face. 'Also, Bulaki, his father … what's his name, Surjan?'

'Dhanu Singh.'

'His father is a soldier and he does not want Surjan to be a painter. He may come looking for him. Tell him …'

'… no Surjan lives here.' The boy ended his sentence.

Bulaki's sharp eyes had spotted the bruise under the boy's left eye. 'Beats you, does he?'

Surjan nodded, suddenly becoming subdued again.

Something occurred to Sayyid Ali. 'How will you meet your mother and sister? They must be very worried by now.'

'I'll go home when my father is on guard duty. He guards the haramsara palace of the Rajput queens and his duty is from noon to sunset.'

Bulaki was holding out a broom. 'Get to work!'

Sayyid Ali settled in his corner on a thick cushion with a big bolster at his back, and pulled the low table closer. On it was a sheet of paper on which he had just begun to sketch out his next painting. He picked up a stick of charcoal and brooded, looking at the blank sheet, letting his mind slow down to the dreamy state in which the images began to float in. It was going to be a hunting scene with the Badshah on a horse, surrounded by his courtiers and with soldiers leading Akbar's pet cheetahs on chains.

Later that morning Surjan bent and touched Basawan's feet as Sayyid Ali said, 'I have a shagird for you, Basawan. Meet Surjan Singh of Amber.'

Surjan looked at Basawan and thought, 'What a wonderful face! He is all darkness and light.' Basawan had a broad nose, fleshy lips and large droopy eyes below bushy eyebrows. His skin was very dark, the shade of ebony against which his eyes gleamed a clear white. He wore sparkling white clothes and even his turban was white. Surjan also noticed that Basawan did not smile.

'Why am I getting a student when you found him?' Basawan asked in a surprisingly mellow, deep voice. 'I have a lot of work to do.'

'And Surjan can help you if you teach him well,' Sayyid Ali's calm voice said. 'No arguments.'

Without another word Basawan turned and headed to his table, with a nervous Surjan shuffling behind him.

'Today you'll just watch and fetch things for me. And you do *not* talk.'

'Ji Ustad.' A nervous pause. 'Can I ask questions?'

The large eyeballs swivelled towards him. 'You may.'

Soon the other artists wandered in, and there were five of them working in the room. Surjan was introduced to them, and as he bent and touched their feet, he heard a lot of bantering about the way he had got Sayyid Ali's attention. There was Hussain Naqqash, Mukund, Miskina and Kesu, and they were all working on paintings that would be part of a book about Badshah Akbar called the *Akbarnama* that had been written by the Badshah's friend Abul Fazl.

'I'm going to prepare a sheet of paper for a painting,' Basawan said. 'Watch carefully because after this you will do it for me.'

Basawan laid a sheet of handmade paper on the table, and using a thick brush, he covered the sheet with a layer of white paint. That puzzled Surjan.

'Ustad,' he whispered, 'can I ask a question?'

Basawan nodded.

'When the paper is white already, why are you painting it white again?'

'The paper soaks up the paint, so we have to create a base on which the colours can be added. Watch me …' As soon as the paint was dry, Basawan picked up a smooth round agate stone and began to rub it carefully over the paint. Surjan realised that the paper now had a pearly white sheen. 'This is called burnishing.'

'Oh yes. This shade of white is so much better.'

'So keep quiet and watch.'

All morning that was all Surjan did. Watch. He would go and sit behind a painter and study what they were doing. Miskina was carefully painting a woman wearing gorgeous clothes, sitting on a terrace. She wore a transparent peshwaz robe over tight trousers and a small blouse. He coloured them in shades of turquoise and gold. Surjan was amazed at how, with a few strokes of white, he drew the peshwaz and made it look transparent.

Hussain was finishing the faces of a scene of Akbar in court, and as the painting was so small, he was using the thinnest brush Surjan had ever seen to draw the eyebrows and lips. Kesu was painting a border of delicate flowers and leaves around a painting. Mukund was busy sketching a dancing girl with her skirts flaring around her. Then Basawan taught him the way to grind and mix paint, and he ran about changing the water in the paint bowls and trimming the brushes.

All the while Sayyid Ali watched his newest shagird from his corner, noticing how Surjan was lost in the world of lines and colours. He would sit still and watch an artist at work with such concentration, it was as if he had forgotten to breathe.

'And that father of his wanted him to pick up a sword,' thought Sayyid Ali. 'Fool!'

As the sun dipped in the west and the natural light faded, the painters put away their things and headed home. Surjan brought in candles in silver holders. Bulaki sent Surjan off to the market to buy vegetables, and then they sat and cooked dinner.

Surjan sniffed a little, chopping an onion, and asked, 'Why doesn't Ustad Basawan smile, Bulaki Dada?'

Bulaki grinned. 'He is a serious man, but Sayyid Ali Ustad says he is among the most talented in the studio.'

'He taught me to burnish the paper and grind paint. When will I be allowed to draw and paint?'

'Not for weeks.'

'Ohhh …' he sighed impatiently.

Surjan's bed was a mattress and a smelly quilt on the floor of the studio, and as he slid in, he realised he was very tired. So much had happened in just one day. He had never expected Ustad Sayyid Ali to notice his drawings and then choose him for a *shagird*! That was beyond his wildest dreams. Then he remembered his mother and sister and thought, 'Amma will be worried; Rajjo will cry. I have to go and meet them tomorrow.' And then Surjan fell asleep.

Next day, an hour after noon, Surjan headed out towards the soldiers' quarters. Ustad Sayyid Ali was right; it was a long way from the karkhana. As he walked along the narrow lane with houses on both sides, he realised that this was a very unusual locality because there were many types of karkhanas on either side of the narrow lane. This was the mohalla of the artists and craftsmen of the kingdom.

He strolled along the lane, peering through the doors into large rooms or courtyards, and discovered that in one karkhana men sat at huge looms weaving carpets. The room was full of rolls of wool and silk in all the colours of the rainbow. In another room, the air was full of tapping and hammering as wood carvers made furniture, doors and window frames. The third had tailors stitching clothes for the royal family, bent over lengths of cloth, their needles flying. The metal karkhana was full of hissing and clanging as swords were being made over a fire, filling the room with smoke.

'What a wonderful place!' he thought dreamily. 'Artists and craftsmen everywhere.' And then he decided, 'I want to stay here forever.'

Surjan chose a route that took him away from the haramsara palaces where he knew his father would be on guard duty. He walked behind the dargah of Sheikh Salim Chishti past the palace called Rang Mahal where they said

Prince Salim was born, and then behind the tall and airy Panch Mahal where the queens sat behind screens to enjoy the breeze. Then he climbed a wall and dropped into an open space where the Badshah played chaugan, with all the players riding horses and pushing a ball about, using a long stick.

Walking across the grass he remembered one match with Akbar on a brown horse and because he was Surjan, he remembered the colours of the clothes that Akbar wore—a light blue jacket over white pyjamas. He had seen Akbar many times because the Badshah liked walking about supervising the work of building and also seemed to enjoy chatting with people. Surjan had noticed that he often wore white or pale colours.

'One day I'll do a painting of the Badshah playing chaugan and I'll make him wear sparkling white clothes and a deep blue patka belt,' Surjan brooded, 'and around him will be other players in maroon and gold, leaf green and silver.'

The row of whitewashed houses where the families of soldiers lived was behind the army barracks. As he neared the house, his sister, eleven year old Rajjo, came running out, crying with relief, 'Oh bhaiya! Where were you?'

His mother was sitting on a charpai in the sun stitching a quilt. She looked up calmly. 'I knew you had run away again. You do that every time your father hits you.' But this time Surjan had so much to tell them and they listened to his adventures as his mother cooked lunch. In the afternoon, his heart light with happiness, he headed back to the studio.

His last words to his mother were, 'Do you know, Amma, Sayyid Ali Ustad says he'll give me a salary.'

'How much?'

'Oh!' he looked startled. 'I don't know. I forgot to ask!' This made her laugh. 'But Amma, I'll be earning, so you and Rajjo can come and stay with me.'

'We shall see,' she stroked his cheek. 'I'll tell your father you have run away to Agra. After a few days he'll stop asking.'

On the long walk back, Surjan thought about his father's endless anger. Why was he always so full of rage? Nothing pleased him; he did not like anyone and had no friends. He even disliked the Badshah! Surjan had once overheard him talking to another Rajput soldier about Akbar marrying Jodh Bai, the Princess of Amber. Dhanu Singh had come to Agra with her entourage.

'I shouldn't have come here,' Dhanu complained. 'A Hindu princess marrying a Muslim king is wrong.'

'The princess is happy enough,' the soldier had protested. 'She is the mother of the heir apparent, Prince Salim, and now has the royal title of Mariam us Zamani. The Badshah has built a separate palace for her where she lives like a Hindu.'

'So what? He is still a Muslim!'

'Our Prince Man Singh of Amber has been made a general in the army. Raja Todar Mal is a senior official in the Treasury and Raja Birbal is the Badshah's friend.' The man was now sounding a bit irritated. 'If these great Hindus can be loyal to him, what's your problem?'

Not having an answer, Dhanu Singh had fallen silent.

'And now I'm working in the studio of the ustads Mir Sayyid Ali and Khwaja Abdus Samad, who are not just Muslims but also from Persia,' Surjan brooded. 'I wonder what he would think of that!'

Then Surjan stopped to watch a row of women pulling water out of a well. He spotted three shades of red, a lehenga in magenta worn with a lemon yellow chunari and then a boy who had amazingly beautiful light grey eyes. He forgot all about his father. The colours and shapes of the world around him were always so much more interesting.

Even though Basawan did not approve, soon enough Surjan began to talk because the other artists asked him so many questions. His chatter kept them entertained as they spent long hours bent over their tables, working on those small, delicate paintings. Soon they all knew Surjan's life story.

'Tell that stupid father of yours,' said Miskina, 'that we painters earn much more than a soldier.'

'It's not the money, Ustad.' Surjan was busy scrubbing a board smeared with streaks of paint. 'He is all about being a proud Rajput and how Rajputs are only soldiers. It is the manly thing to do.'

'So what are we?' Hussain asked, amused.

'Sissies!' Surjan grinned. 'He said I wanted to be a painter because I was too scared to fight.'

'Hah!' Basawan finally spoke. 'I can use a sword. Anyone can wave one around.'

'You can fight with a sword, Ustad?' Surjan widened his eyes. 'Will you teach me?'

'First learn to hold a brush. It is harder.'

As the days went by, Surjan watched a miniature painting appear under Basawan's hand. He was doing a painting of the Badshah in court and first he sketched the outline in faint charcoal lines. He placed the Badshah on his throne, then the people before him, the courtiers, attendants and soldiers. Then, using the thinnest of brushes, he began to fill in the colours. The patterns on the carpet, the gorgeous clothes, the wall hangings, the golden throne ...

Finally he picked up a brush with only a few bristles, dipped it in the black paint and very slowly drew Akbar's face. With tiny, firm strokes he drew the winged eyebrows, the drooping moustaches over the firm lips and the large eyes. Soon Jalaluddin Akbar was staring back at them. Surjan, who had been watching breathlessly, gave a small sigh of satisfaction.

For the first time, Basawan smiled. 'Like it?'

'Oh yes, Ustad. It is perfect!'

'Tomorrow you can start doing some drawings.' And then he laughed as the young face before him lit up in delight.

In the beginning, Surjan sketched to learn, copying the work of the mussawirs. He used the backs of scraps of paper discarded by the artists and practiced drawing people and animals, flowers and trees, clouds and flocks of flying birds. And Basawan would study them critically and point out his mistakes. He would make Surjan draw them again and again till his hand and eye began to move with perfect coordination.

One day Surjan sat watching Kesu paint a monsoon scene with the trees bent by the wind and grey clouds scudding across the sky. He asked, 'Ustad, how will you paint raindrops?'

'Like strings of small pearls falling from the sky,' said Kesu, and Surjan knew exactly what he meant.

It was Friday, the day of prayers, and the studio was closed. After lunch, Surjan wandered off to the bazaar at the bottom of the hill. That morning Ustad Sayyid Ali had given him his first salary and he was feeling rich. He stood at a stall selling cloth, planning to buy some for a kurta for himself and a blouse for Rajjo.

Suddenly a heavy hand landed on his shoulder and grabbed his arm. 'There you are! I knew you were not in Agra!' Surjan froze in panic, his heart beginning to race as he turned to see his father standing behind him. Dhanu Singh's fleshy, moustached face was already flushed with anger. 'I knew your mother was lying. When you run away, she cries. This time she was looking too happy.'

His father was gripping his arm so hard, it hurt. 'Baba, please!' As Surjan tried to wriggle out of his clutches, a hard slap hit his cheek.

'You are coming with me!' Dhanu Singh began to hit him right there, punching and slapping Surjan and making his head ring. Then he began to drag Surjan out of the bazaar. 'Just you wait! I'm going to beat you black and blue ...'

In his desperation, Surjan turned and bit his father's hand. With a yell of surprise Dhanu let go of his arm. Surjan slid away and started running as fast as his legs would carry him. As he ran, he could hear his father's rapid steps behind him. He thought in desperation, 'I can't go towards the studio or he'll know where I stay.' He blindly turned in the opposite direction from the tasvir khana into a narrow lane and ran smack into a man coming towards him.

'Oof! Look where you are going!' a deep voice said in protest as a pair of hands held him steady. Surjan looked up into a smiling face with plump cheeks, a droopy moustache and amused eyes. 'What's the hurry, boy?'

'He'll kill me, huzoor!'

'Who?'

'My father!'

'Not while I am here.'

By then a panting Dhanu had turned the corner and entered the lane. As he came hurrying towards them, Surjan slid behind the man and whispered, 'That's him, huzoor!'

'Stop!' said the man in a loud voice. To Surjan's astonishment, he saw his father take a look at the man's face and slide to a stop. Then Dhanu bowed deeply and exclaimed, 'Raja Sa'ab!'

'What's your name, soldier?'

'Dhanu Singh, huzoor. I'm stationed at the haramsara.'

'Is this boy your son?'

Dhanu nodded.

'Why are you chasing him?'

'He ran away, Raja Sa'ab. He's a very disobedient boy and I ...'

Surjan, quite astonished at his father's change in behaviour, had got his breath back. He whispered from behind the man's back, 'Huzoor, who are you?'

The man laughed. 'They call me Birbal.' And Surjan promptly bent and touched his feet as Birbal asked, 'So why did you run away?'

'He's always been a very troublesome boy and ...' Dhanu began.

'I'm speaking to your son.' There was a hint of steel in Birbal's voice. 'I want to hear what he has to say.'

Birbal's kind face gave Surjan courage and he said in a rush, 'He hits me and my mother and sister all the time. And

Rajjo is so small ... He is angry with me because he wants me to be a soldier even though I want to be a painter ...'

'No Rajput becomes a painter. Painters are not real men!' Dhanu interrupted Surjan angrily.

'Well, Dhanu Singh, I write poetry,' Birbal said mildly. 'What do you think I am?' Surjan's father fell silent. 'Real men hit women and children, do they?'

'Ustad Sayyid Ali has taken me as his shagird,' Surjan explained, 'and I'm working at the karkhana. My father does not like that.'

'Oh, you are the boy who drew on the walls! Sayyid Ali was telling me about you.' Birbal turned to Dhanu. 'You will go back to your barracks, soldier. And remember, this boy is now under my protection. You will stay away from him.' Dhanu's face was flushed with anger but he did not have the courage to protest. As he turned to go away, Birbal said firmly, 'And soldier, if I hear that you have hit anyone in your family again, I'll have you in chains. So be careful!'

Without another word, Dhanu Singh strode away. Surjan bent down and touched Birbal's feet.

'What? Again? I'm feeling like a god in a temple!' Birbal laughed. Then as he turned to leave, he said, 'Surjan, tell Ustad Sayyid Ali I'll be at the studio tomorrow morning. I need his advice.'

As he headed back to the bazaar, Surjan's heart was singing with happiness. There was a bruise on his arm where his father had held him. His cheeks were red from the slaps, but oh, the joy! He was free!

'He will never have the courage to stand up to Raja Birbal,' Surjan thought about his father. 'Ammi is right. He only bullies people who can't fight back. He is a coward who is always bowing and scraping before the rich,' he sighed. 'Now I have to start saving my salary and rent a room where Amma and Rajjo can stay with me.'

Next morning Birbal strolled into the studio saying that he wanted to see the paintings being done for the manuscript called *Akbarnama*. This was a history of Badshah Akbar's reign being written by the royal historian Abul Fazl Allami. The pages were being illustrated by the mussawirs. He settled on a cushion and leaned back against a bolster, ready to have a good time.

'Abul Fazl writes the history of the Badshah,' Birbal gave a theatrical sigh, 'and I write funny poems! That's why no one takes me seriously.'

'I think you are a great poet, huzoor,' Abdus Samad smiled. 'And making the Badshah laugh? Now that is an important job!'

'Ah yes,' Birbal nodded, 'it is called being a jester.' And everyone in the room began to laugh. Surjan came in with a plate of sweets and a glass of sherbet and then sat down quietly behind Sayyid Ali.

'Surjan tells me you need my advice,' Sayyid Ali said. 'How can I help you, Raja Sa'ab?'

'Next week is Prince Salim's fifth birthday and you know that a huge celebration is being planned. Now can you suggest a present that I can give him? What will a five-year-old boy like?'

All the painters had their own ideas.

'Maybe a poem or a song?' Mukund suggested.

'A silk peshwaz and patka.' Miskina said.

'A silver bowl for his milk?' Hussain Naqqash asked.

'A horse?' Kesu joined in.

'A portrait of the boy? I could do one, huzoor,' Basawan asked.

'Hmmm … others will also give such gifts. Think about it.' Birbal got up to leave. 'Something for a prince who has everything.'

A week later Surjan stood at the gate of Birbal's haveli holding a strangely-shaped bundle in his arm. 'I have come from the tasvir khana of Mir Sayyid Ali,' he told the gateman. 'There is a packet for Raja Sa'ab.'

He was ushered into Birbal's baithak where the raja was sitting on a mattress laid on the floor, surrounded by rolls of paper, busy with the work of the kingdom. 'Ah, my runaway friend! You have something for me?'

'My name's Surjan Singh, huzoor,' he reminded him, 'and I have some gifts for Prince Salim.'

Surjan opened the bundle and took out toys and laid them out in a row before Birbal. They were elephants, horses, camels all carved out of wood and painted in shiny bright colours. The elephants had their trunks raised high, the camels had smiling faces and the horses had raised front legs as if they were marching.

'The prince will lead his army one day, so this is his toy one.'

Birbal clapped his hands in delight. 'This is exactly what I wanted! Sayyid Ali made these? I didn't know he was a wood carver too.'

'No huzoor, I made them. I was working in the wood carver's karkhana for the last few days. We have toys like these in Amber.'

'You are a genius, Surjan.'

Surjan gave a modest smile. 'I'm good with my hands.'

Surjan's way back took him past the haramsara and he caught a glimpse of his father standing at the entrance. Just then Dhanu Singh turned his head and saw him. Sarju saw his hands reach towards his sword. If Dhanu thought this would scare his son, he was mistaken. Even though his mouth was dry and his heart thudding, Sarju did not run away. He stared back at his father and walked on with calm, measured steps. Before turning the corner, he turned to look back. Dhanu still stood there, as if frozen, his face dark with rage.

'He does not have the courage to come after me,' thought Surjan, 'and he never will.' Then he skipped with joy. 'I have to tell Amma about this!'

It was summer and the sun came out early, so Surjan would leave his bed at dawn and wander around Fatehpur Sikri. He was in agreement with Ustad Sayyid Ali—this was the best time of the day to draw and dream. He carried a bundle of paper and sketched anything that caught his eye—the arch of a gateway, the curve of a tree branch with a squirrel sitting on it, the carved pillar of a haveli, a long-haired beggar …'

This morning he was sitting in the courtyard of the mosque they called Jami Masjid. Right before him was the dargah of Sheikh Salim Chisti. Surjan loved this quiet, serene courtyard and came here often. He loved the way the marble dargah gleamed, surrounded by the red sandstone mosque. During daytime it was full of people who came to pray at the grave of the Sufi saint, but it was empty now. Only some pigeons and sparrows were pecking about around him, and he was sketching the birds.

'That's a very pretty pigeon,' a voice spoke behind him. He looked up to see a very familiar royal face.

'Your Majesty!' Surjan sprang up, the paper and charcoal scattering around him as he bowed.

'Sit!' said King Jalaluddin Akbar briskly. 'Go on drawing.' And then he took a sheet of paper, picked up a piece of charcoal, sat down and said, 'I think I'll draw too. And what is your name?' he looked up at Surjan still standing there uncertainly and said briskly, 'Sit! Here, beside me.'

'Surjan, sir.' Very carefully, Surjan sat down beside the king. Feeling nervous and excited, he went back to sketching.

Akbar took a closer look at the bent face and at what he was sketching. Then his said suddenly, 'Aren't you Sayyid Ali's new shagird, the one who drew on the walls?'

Surjan gave him a startled glance. 'How did you know that, sir?'

'Birbal told me when he brought those toys for Salim.' Akbar was now sitting cross-legged beside Surjan who was busy scribbling. He realised he wasn't feeling nervous any more. He glanced down and saw that Akbar had begun to draw a tree.

'One day,' said Akbar broodingly, 'I'm going to become Sayyid Ali's shagird just like you.'

Surjan grinned. 'But you are the king.'

'I can build walls with bricks, dig the earth for a garden, carve wood and even weave a little.'

'You're good with your hands,' Surjan said solemnly.

'That is correct.'

For a while the man and boy sat peaceably sketching, not saying a word. Then Akbar spoke. 'Salim loves those toys. He plays with them all the time.'

'Then I'll make some more—soldiers, cats, dancers …' Surjan paused and then asked tentatively, 'Sir, can I ask you something?'

'Yes you can.'

'Without fear?'

Akbar raised his head to look at him. 'Without any fear.'

'You are a Muslim and Prince Salim's mother is a Hindu …'

'Yes.' Akbar was now adding mangoes to his tree.

'And Prince Salim?'

'He is a Muslim who will one day marry a Hindu princess. I'm thinking of Man Singh's sister, Man Bai.'

'But he's only five years old!'

'She is three. They will match well.' A small smile peeped out from behind the drooping moustache. Then he turned to study Surjan's puzzled face. 'They will marry when they grow up, of course. He will be the king one day, so he has to understand all the religions of this kingdom. His wife will teach him about Hindus. Otherwise how will he keep his subjects united?'

Surjan had pulled out a fresh sheet of paper and begun a new sketch. His hand moving quickly over the paper.

'I pray five times a day,' Akbar went on, staring absently before him. 'I also play Holi, beat the drums at Dussehra and like wearing a tika. Like the Persians, I worship the fire, celebrate Navroz and every morning I say a prayer to the sun.' Then he nodded towards the dargah. 'But most of all I pray to him, my Sheikhji. He is my Pir and I am his murid.'

Surjan was listening and sketching rapidly.

'Sheikhji said you just have to pray with love and devotion. It doesn't matter what you call god—Allah or Ram or Vishnu.'

'Then can I make a toy Krishna for Prince Salim?'

Akbar threw back his head and laughed. 'Ah, that is why you were asking! Of course you can! It will make his mother very happy.' Then as Surjan leaned across and took a closer look at Akbar's tree, he asked, 'What do you think?'

Surjan cleared his throat and said a little apologetically, 'Sir, you have drawn mangoes but the leaves are like those of a neem tree. And that duck floating in the pond has a very strange beak.'

'Ah well,' Akbar put away the drawing with a sigh. 'I'll leave it to you then. But don't forget your next gift for Salim. I want a smiling baby Krishna.'

As Akbar got up to go, Surjan handed him the sheet on which he had been drawing. 'This is for you, sir.'

'For me?' Akbar looked down at a quickly drawn portrait of his face, as he sat beside Surjan, his face lowered, busy drawing. Surjan had caught all the details of his face, the high cheekbones, the arching eyebrows, the sharp nose with flared nostrils, a small mole below it and the firm, well-formed lips. 'Oh, this is a very good likeness, Surjan. Thank you! Can I take it? I want to show it to Birbal.'

'One day, sir, I'll paint you playing chaugan.'

As Akbar turned to leave, Sarju exclaimed suddenly, 'Oh I forgot!' and bent and touched his feet.

'What was that for?' Akbar asked, startled.

'Because you are my king and I'm a painter today because of you.'

With a smile, Akbar touched his head in blessing. For Sarju that quick stroke of his hand on his head was like a benediction from heaven.

Then Surjan stood and watched the short stocky man, carrying a roll of paper, walk briskly away.

HISTORICAL NOTE

The Mughal emperor Jalaluddin Akbar built a new city near Agra called Fatehpur Sikri where he set up many studios and workshops. Among them the most famous was the mussawir's karkhana where the miniature painters worked, illustrating manuscripts like the Akbarnama, Ain-i-Akbari and even the Mahabharata.

Akbar's father Humayun had brought two Persian painters to India—Mir Sayyid Ali and Khwaja Abdus Samad, and they established this studio in Fatehpur Sikri. All the painters mentioned in the story, Basawan, Mukund, Hussain Naqqash, Kesu and Miskina, worked on the Akbarnama, and many of their paintings have survived till today. The story of Surjan is an imaginary one but it is inspired by the true story of Daswant. He was the son of a poor kahar, a palki bearer, and Akbar discovered him. Daswant was drawing on the walls of his hut when the Mughal king was wandering around incognito in Agra. Daswant later became a famous painter. In Akbar's world it was your talent and abilities that were given value, not whether you were rich or poor, lower caste or upper caste, Hindu or Muslim. He united his kingdom because he was a true Indian king.

LISTENING TO A PRINCESS

She had many names in the royal harem. Some of the royal women called her "Chhoti" like they called all the young maids because they couldn't be bothered to remember the names of servants. Others called out to her roughly, 'Eh ladki!' as if being a young girl somehow made her nameless, while some would just wave imperiously and then give their orders.

Only Princess Jahanara always called her by her real name. She never forgot. She would smile slightly and say courteously, 'Sakina Bano, will you fetch my woollen shawl from the bedroom please?' Or turn to a guest and say, 'And this is my most loyal companion, Sakina Bano. She is young but very clever.'

That is what makes her a real princess, Sakina often thought. Not because she was a royal Mughal, not even because she was Emperor Shahjahan's eldest daughter and a noble and titled lady, but because she was kind and courteous, generous and caring. She had the heart and soul of a true princess.

It was easy to be forgotten in the Mughal harem with so many queens and princesses living there. In the Red Fort in Delhi, Shahjahan had built many marble palaces, and among them some of the most beautiful were reserved for the harem. These palaces were hidden behind high hedges and guarded by soldiers, and no men were allowed inside these palaces except those belonging to the Mughal family. There were hundreds of women there, old and young, queens and princesses, aunts and cousins, and all of them had maids and companions. So Sakina was just one among many women working there. She was nothing special. Except that Princess Jahanara made her feel special.

For the princess she was always a real girl who was called Sakina. She knew all about Sakina's family and asked her often about them. She called Sakina her "companion" and not her youngest and lowliest maid who was just fourteen years old. And the princess never forgot anything. She would check every day that Sakina had eaten her breakfast before coming to work, that she had enough warm clothes and shoes in winter and new angrakhas and dupattas in summer. If Sakina was unwell, the princess would get the hakim to prescribe medicines and then would make sure Sakina took them.

As the other maids told her, she was very lucky to work for Jahanara. The other royal women were never so kind. Many maids were beaten by bad-tempered queens or given old and torn clothes to wear. Even the princess's younger sister Roshanara was known for her quick temper and she scolded her maids so much that they kept quitting. Roshanara even told Jahanara that she spoilt Sakina when maids needed to be disciplined, and Jahanara just laughed. Sakina wanted to take care of her princess for her whole life.

Everyone thought the princess must lead an easy and luxurious life, but Sakina knew how hard she worked. When her mother Begum Mumtaz Mahal died, Jahanara was just eighteen years old, and since then she had been the head of the harem. All day she was busy making sure it ran properly. Everyone who worked there came to report to her—the head chef, the seniormost of the maids, the store keeper, the head gardener, the teachers, the singers, the painters ... and because this was the royal harem, all of them were women.

On most days, the princess' father Shahjahan often came to Jahanara's palace to have his lunch, so she had to decide on a menu with the cooks. She checked all the accounts and made sure everyone was given their salary and the bills were paid. Then there were the fights among the women that she had to sort out and Jahanara would sit on a throne and pass judgement about their disputes.

Also, the princess had a very important role as her father's adviser on running the kingdom. She held the royal seal that had to be placed on all the firmans, the royal orders. So, bunches of these orders written on rolls of paper would arrive at her palace every day. Often she and her father would sit and discuss the firmans after Jahanara had read them and only after she had placed the seal on the paper would Shahjahan sign them.

It wasn't easy being the Begum Sahiba, the head of the haramsara, the Mughal harem.

Sakina's job was to be like a shadow of her princess. She would be there when Jahanara asked for a glass of water or a soft cushion for her back. When she needed something to be fetched or someone had to be summoned, Sakina would run to help her. Jahanara said that Sakina was very good at reading her mind, otherwise how did she know what Jahanara needed even before she had said it out aloud?

And Sakina would laugh and reply, 'No my princess, I can read your face. I knew your back was aching from sitting over those papers for so long.'

Sakina knew that the best time for the princess was at night, when all her day's work was done and all the lamps in the palaces went out. She would settle before her low table and pick up her books as Sakina lit the candles. Sakina, who could barely write her name, never knew what her princess found so enjoyable in those fat books. Their pages were filled with lines of writing that made her head ache, but she did like the beautiful paintings on the facing pages. Jahanara would read late into the night and Sakina, waiting up for her, would often curl up in a corner of the mattress on the floor and fall asleep. She would wake up again when Jahanara finally closed her book and blew out the candles. Then, sleepy-eyed and yawning, she would help the princess to bed.

***

That night Jahanara turned to her and said, 'Sakina, did you remember to fill the ink bottle and sharpen the quill pens?'

'Ji Begum Sahiba,' she said and gave a sparkling smile as she carried the low table to place it before Jahanara. 'You're going to write tonight?'

'Yes,' Jahanara pushed back the sleeves of her angrakha, took off a big ring she wore on a finger of her right hand and picked up a quill. She dipped it into the glass bottle filled with black ink. 'I feel like writing something. Some lines have been running in my head since morning and I have to write them down before I forget.'

'Will it be poetry today, Begum Sahiba?' asked Sakina, putting a warm shawl around her shoulders and placing a large bolster at her back. 'Some nazms or a ghazal perhaps?'

Jahanara laughed. 'A ghazal, I think. You like that, don't you?'

'Yes!' sighed Sakina happily.

That was the best of all, when the princess composed a ghazal and then sang it softly to her. All those lovely lyrics about flowers and birds, love and parting, floating clouds

and a curving moon and then the poem was sung in the soft mellow voice of the princess.

'You are the best ghazal singer in the world!' Sakina said loyally, making Jahanara shake her head and smile.

Sakina sat in the corner of the room, absently watching as Jahanara bent low over the sheet of paper and began to write. Jahanara thought for a while, her delicate brows furrowed, scribbled a bit, scratched out some lines and then wrote some more. She hummed softly under her breath and wrote again as her pet cat wandered in and went and curled up in Jahanara's lap. Beginning to feel cold, Sakina wrapped herself in a warm blanket. Slowly her eyes closed and she drifted off to sleep. Her last image was of Jahanara's beautiful face lit by candlelight, bent over the table as her pen wrote swiftly on the creamy yellow paper.

When Sakina woke up, it was morning. She scrambled up, thinking in horror, 'Oh Allah! I did not wake up when the princess went to bed!' She glanced out of the door and realised that it was still very early and the sun was hidden behind the mist that lay like smoke around the gardens. The palaces were still and quiet; only the maids were sweeping the courtyards and dusting the rooms. So she had some time to clear up the room before she went in to wake the princess.

She went up to Jahanara's table and saw that the princess had written a long poem and left it there for the ink to dry. It was as she bent to put away the papers that she saw the gold ring. Jahanara had taken it off before she had begun to write, and now it lay forgotten among the pens and papers. Sakina picked it up and stood looking at it. It was shaped like a rose with glittering diamonds set along the gold petals. A big glowing red ruby was set in the heart of the flower. It was so beautiful!

Without thinking, Sakina slipped the ring on her finger and held her hand out to study it. The ring was a bit loose, but suddenly her hand looked so elegant and pretty! Just like the hand of a princess. With a guilty start she took off the ring and tied it to a corner of her dupatta. She went on with the cleaning and dusting of the room.

Later, as Sakina helped Jahanara dress, she realised that the princess had forgotten about the ring. Jahanara was sitting before her mirror and she was busy talking about the song she had written. 'I finished the ghazal and then I thought I'd sing it to you, but you were fast asleep.'

Sakina was combing and plaiting her long hair and said, 'You should have woken me up, Begum Sahiba. I really did want to hear the ghazal. I am so sorry I fell asleep!'

'It was very late, and the whole haramsara was asleep, my dear.' Sakina knew the princess found it difficult to fall asleep at night. 'The only people who were awake to listen to my ghazal were the guards at the gate and I don't think they were interested.' And they exchanged a swift amused glance in the mirror.

Sakina watched Jahanara open her jewellery box and stare thoughtfully at the gems inside, and her heart began to thud. Then the princess reached into the box and took out a pair of diamond bangles, an emerald ring and matching earrings and a necklace, all the while humming her new ghazal under her breath. Sakina gave a soft sigh of relief but suddenly the ring tied to the edge of her dupatta felt as heavy as a large stone. She opened her mouth to speak, but before she could say anything, another maid came in, saying that an old queen was ill and asking for the princess. Jahanara went out quickly.

Sakina sat on the steps, leaning against a pillar outside the palace, brooding. 'She does not even remember about the ring. She has boxes of jewellery and won't even miss it. But I have nothing so pretty. I will never ever have anything like it. I could wear it when I go to the Eid bazaar and to weddings. I just have to make sure the princess does not see me wearing it.' Then, squaring her shoulders, she thought, 'I'll keep it. If the princess looks for it then I'll act as if I found it somewhere and give it back. Otherwise the ring is mine.'

All day Sakina carried the ring around, still tied to her dupatta, too scared to take it out. To her surprise, she did not feel happy, and had no appetite at lunch. As Jahanara went about her work in the palace, as always, she followed behind. As they headed for the storeroom where Jahanara was going to check the supplies, she turned and said, 'You're very quiet today. Are you unwell, Sakina?'

'No, Begum Sahiba,' Sakina mumbled.

'I just wondered,' Jahanara flashed a smile at her. 'You usually get an attack of giggles when my stepmother Fatehpuri Begum tells me the same story about her pet parrot again and again ...'

'I did giggle …' Sakina grinned, 'but very very softly …'

'Ah, soft giggles … that's new! Still, if anything is bothering you, you know you can always talk to me.'

'I know, Begum Sahiba.'

***

Late in the afternoon, after His Majesty Shahjahan had gone back to his palace after lunch, Jahanara could finally relax. Sati-un-Nissa Khanum sat with her, chatting with the princess. They sat basking in the sun in the courtyard of her palace and right below the fort wall, the river Yamuna shimmered by the sunlight. Sati-un-Nissa Khanum used to be Mumtaz Mahal's best friend and constant companion, and now she was like an aunt to Jahanara.

As the two women talked about haramsara matters and about Jahanara's brothers and sisters, Sakina thought of how the princess was like a real mother to all of them. She knew everything about their lives. Jahanara glanced at Sakina who was standing behind her chair and said, 'Have you had your lunch?'

'Ji Begum Sahiba.'

'Do you know,' Jahanara said to Sati-un-Nissa, 'that our Sakina Bano now has a soft giggle when Fatehpuri Begum tells that old, old story of her parrot?'

'Oh, that story again! Well, Fatehpuri can't hear anything anyway, so you could giggle as loudly as you want.' And they all laughed.

Jahanara glanced at Sakina's face, pointed to a spot by her feet and said, 'Sit, you must be tired, running after me all day.'

Sakina perched on a cushion at the princess's feet, the sun falling on her face, listening half sleepily to the two women talking away above her. Then she felt Jahanara's hand absently stroke her head. Feeling the gentle fingers on her hair, suddenly Sakina's throat was tight with tears.

It was night again and Sakina was lighting the candles around the room, waiting for the princess to arrive. Jahanara came carrying her notebook of poems and said, 'So do you want to hear my new ghazal or not, Sakina Bano?'

'I do, Begum Sahiba.'

'You usually sound happier.' Jahanara sat on the divan, reclining against cushions, and opened her notebook. Maybe I'll teach you to read and write and then you can compose your own ghazals.'

Sakina leaned forward and put the ruby ring before Jahanara. 'You left this on your writing table last night, Begum Sahiba. I put it away and then forgot to give it back to you. Forgive me.'

Jahanara looked up. Her huge intelligent eyes studied Sakina's flushed and apologetic face and she felt as if they saw right into the girl's mind. 'Thank you for keeping it safe, Sakina.' She reached out and touched Sakina's hot cheek. 'I know I can trust you.'

Suddenly Sakina's heart was as light as a kite soaring high in the sky, as happy as a koel bird singing from the mango tree, as carefree as Jahanara's pet cat when it chased pigeons along the palace walls. For the first time that day she smiled.

Jahanara was watching the flitting expressions on her young face closely and gave an understanding smile. 'Ghazals are better than rings, aren't they, Sakina?' As Sakina nodded, she opened her notebook and began, 'Then listen …'

....

HISTORICAL NOTE

Princess Jahanara was the eldest daughter of the Mughal Emperor Shahjahan who built the Red Fort in Delhi. One part of the fort, reserved for the royal family, has a row of marble palaces called the haramsara where the royal women lived. The palace in the corner called Mumtaz Mahal was Jahanara's palace. Now it is a museum that displays fascinating Mughal artefacts like clothes, furniture, jewellery, arms and armour.

Princess Jahanara was a scholar and poet and was loved by people for her kindness and charity. She was a devotee of the Sufi saint Sheikh Nizamuddin Auliya and her grave is at the mausoleum of the saint in Delhi. The top of her grave is not covered; it has earth on which plants and grass grow because Jahanara, who loved nature, wanted her grave to be open to the sky.

....

OUR VERY OWN FLAG

6 Abdul! Abdoool!' the Memsahib's thin high-pitched voice echoed across the back courtyard of the bungalow.

My heart began to thud as I ran out of the servant's quarters and stood before her. 'Memsahib?'

'Why are you here? I called Abdul, not you,' she snapped at me. It was barely seven in the morning and her face was already screwed up in an irritated frown. 'Where's your father, Bilal?'

'He's gone to the bazaar to buy vegetables, Memsahib.' I hated lying, but then what else could I say? That my father had got roaring drunk last night and could barely walk this morning?

'I bring the morning tea now and Bawarchi Sahib will serve breakfast,' I said.

'Oh alright …' she began walking away. 'Tell him to see me when he's back. I want the hisaab.' And as I was turning away, she added, 'And oh, Bilal … tell the gardener to bring the flowers.'

'Ji Memsahib.'

It looked like this morning I would have to do all of Abbu's work—help with breakfast and do the vegetable shopping. Hopefully by lunchtime Abbu would be able to get up and serve lunch in the dining room.

I knew the pattern of his drinking binges. He'd be tottering about in the morning but somehow he always gathered himself together and looked his usual calm, efficient self by noon. So that when the Sahib's phaeton carriage came through the gate, he would be standing at the main door in his starched white uniform, face impassive, looking like the perfect khansama. Only if you looked closely would you spot the bloodshot eyes and the slight shaking of his hands. Luckily, the binges did not happen very often.

Our bawarchi, or as he liked to call himself, Chef Gomes, often said to Abbu, 'Man, why you go crazy like dat? It is like you get dat worm in your brain or something, man, a drinking worm …'

I strolled into the kitchen and said, 'Chef, I serve morning tea and I help with breakfast, theek hai? And I do veggie shopping today.'

Chef was beating eggs for the omelettes and turned his dark, round sweaty face towards me. 'He drink again, eh, Bilal boy?'

'Ji chef.'

'Theek hai, morning tea is ready, so you take it now. I do breakfast alone and you do veggie shopping. Go get paper and pencil.' And he dictated the shopping list. 'If dat woman ask, I say your papa go to the bazaar, no?' Just like me, Chef knew the drill for covering up for Abbu.

'Thanks Chef.'

"That woman"—that's what we call our revered Memsahib, Mrs Evelyn Montgomery, wife of Rt Hon Richard Montgomery, Chief Magistrate of Amroli in the United Provinces.

Amroli is a small town near the provincial capital Lucknow and this bungalow is in the cantonment, the separate area where all the British lived, away from the main Indian part of town. They live well, these angrez. The cantonment has these large whitewashed bungalows with wide verandahs and gardens, large rooms filled with expensive furniture and an army of servants in the quarters at the back who do all the work. At our bungalow there is the bawarchi or the cook and two assistants in the kitchen; the khansama or major domo, the dhobi or washerman, the mali or gardener, the ayah or maid, the office assistant, the peon, the carriage driver and the syce. Even the poorest among the angrez has at least four servants.

Evelyn Montgomery is the burra mem of our lives whose high-pitched call of "Bilaaaal!" makes me think of the scream of an eagle about to pounce on a baby bird. She has only one purpose in her life—to catch us out. Is Gomes stealing from the spice box? Is my father the khansama Abdul Latif padding the shopping bill? Has the gardener Shivpal sold her mangoes and guavas in the market? Is ayah Dulari sleeping and not ironing the napkins? Have I been helping myself to her marmalade from the dining table?

She is the policeman of our lives and Shivpal chacha calls her Kotwal Mem, a mem police inspector.

Kotwal Mem is tall and thin and wears long trailing skirts in flowery prints, frilly blouses and lots of jangly bangles that don't match her hard, bony face. She never smiles, and her small thin-lipped mouth is always pursed in disapproval. Her tiny, beady brown eyes are cold and there are frown lines etched between her eyebrows. What I hate the most is that high, squeaky voice that always sounds so superior when she speaks to us, as if the servants are somehow not human at all, just stupid cattle she has to whip into shape.

Every time anyone makes a mistake she rolls her eyes and says, 'Oh really?' and then speaks to us very slowly as if she is talking to idiots.

I wandered around the vegetable market picking up cabbages and pumpkins, garlic and potatoes. I selected the vegetables carefully because our chef was a fussy cook and would protest if the tomatoes were soft or the coriander leaves going brown. But then he really was an amazing cook and his chicken vindaloo and mulligatawny soup were famous among the angrez in Amroli. People never refused an invitation to dinner at our bungalow, and the kotwal mem took all the credit.

I am trying to make up my mind if I want to become a khansama like Abbu or a bawarchi like Chef Gomes. Stirring up a handi of mutton korma or jhalfrezie could be more fun that polishing the cutlery and laying the table. Though I quite enjoy serving the guests at dinner, the candlelight and conversation, the fragrance of flowers and perfume do make dinner parties exciting events.

As I had known, Abbu was on his feet by noon. 'Did that woman call me?'

'Ji! She wants the market hisaab for last week.'

'She would,' Abbu grunted.

Ammi, who was sitting there putting buttons on my kurta, looked up and asked Abbu, 'You didn't take any money from the house expenses, did you?'

He turned his bloodshot eyes towards her. 'Why would you think that?'

'You drank *again* last night.'

'With my own money!' he glared at her, which had no effect, as she calmly went on stitching.

Right on the dot of 1:15 in the afternoon Abbu and I stood at the door waiting for the phaeton carriage to stop in the porch. Sahib stepped out, or rather his belly came out first, followed by his red face with the bushy brown moustache under a sola topi. He took small steps, wiping the sweat on his round face. Sahib does not screech like his wife—he grunts.

'Ugh … Bilal … gah … there are papers in there.' He waved to the carriage. 'Take them to the study …' I clambered in, picked up the bundle of files and followed Sahib and Abbu inside, listening to them talk.

Sahib asks the same two questions everyday. 'Lunch ready, Abdul?'

'Ji Sahib.'

Question number two—here it comes. 'Anyone coming for dinner?'

'Ji. Chhota Magistrate Sahib and his Mem, Major Sahib and his Mem, and Paadri Sahib.'

'Ahh … good … ugh …'

Chef says that Sahib invites people over for dinner because then he wouldn't have to listen to the complaints of the Kotwal Mem. Abbu, who has been working for him for years, says he's not really a bad man, and just likes being left in peace with his whiskey and cigars.

Just then Kotwal Mem came hurrying out, flapping a hand fan as though she had been working hard all morning, when all she had done was arrange flowers, drink tea and write some letters.

'Oh Reggie … there is a letter from home …'

'In a … ugh … minute, Evie …' he said.

In the evening Abbu and I were busy setting the table for dinner. We first spread the thick damask tablecloth on the dining table and then laid out the bone china crockery with the design of blue flowers. First the dinner plates, then the soup plates, the side plates, the big bowls, small bowls … then the many kinds of glasses—for wine, claret and water. Finally Abbu opened the cutlery drawer and began placing the forks, spoons and knives for soup, fish, meat and dessert.

I studied the row of shining silver cutlery and sighed. 'Small fork, big fork, small spoon, big spoon and then the knives … I still can't get them right. Abbu, how is it that we Indians just need a plate and a bowl to eat and they need so many things?' We always spoke in Hindustani when discussing the angrez inside the bungalow. Luckily for us, our mem and the Sahib have never bothered to learn Hindustani. The only word they knew was "Koi hai?"

'Because they don't know how to eat with their hands. Why would Allah give us hands if you were not supposed to eat with them?'

'Chef says that they chew the cutlery instead of the chicken bones,' and that made Abbu laugh, and I knew he was not feeling gloomy anymore.

That night I stood at the door waiting for the guests. First to arrive was the priest from the church, Reverend John Abbot, then came the deputy magistrate Edmond Shore and his wife Emily, and finally Major Brennan and his wife Charlotte. I bowed and opened the door and wished them good evening. Only the Reverend bothered to reply. The others swept past as if I did not exist. They came for dinner every week and none of them knew my name.

It was close to eleven when they wandered into the dining room and Abbu and I could start serving dinner. All of them had flushed faces and unsteady steps from the drinks and were talking loudly and laughing even louder. Kotwal Mem's high-pitched laugh made my ears ache.

'Oh Evie, you should have been there! You would have been in splits,' Shore Sahib was saying. 'That lawyer Srivastava had such trouble pronouncing simple words like "judicial review" and "habeas corpus". They all laughed as he mimicked the poor man.

'Ah, I once heard that man Gandhi give a speech,' Rev Abbot added. 'He speaks like the coolie lawyer that he used to be.'

'Have you heard what Churchill calls him?' Major Brennan asked. 'The naked faqir!' And there was another burst of laughter. 'I really don't understand. Does that man have no shame, wandering around just in a loincloth?'

'I hear they are planning another protest,' Mrs Shore said. 'Is he going on another march now?'

'Oh, I wish he would,' our Sahib grunted. 'I'd hoped the Dandi March would finish him. He's much older now and … gah … he won't survive it this time. And good riddance.'

'Oh Reggie!' Kotwal Mem screamed. 'You're so wicked.'

Abbu and I stood there, listening. As always, we were invisible to them as they made fun of Indians as if we were barbarians. Is it because we have dark skin and we do not speak English correctly? They do not speak our languages well either, but that is fine? And why was Gandhiji always called "that coolie lawyer" or that "old man"? And would our Sahib really be happy if Gandhiji died?

Next morning I went in search of the one person who could answer my questions—my friend Murari. He reads the newspapers. He was the son of the gardener Shivpal chacha and he was a few years older than me. Also, he was lucky chacha had let him go to school so that this year he had given the Matric exams. I had just passed my class 8 examination when Abbu yanked me out of school and put me to work as his assistant. I wanted to study, and Ammi supported me, but he had convinced Sahib to give me a small salary. And for Abbu, money always came first. So two years ago, at the age of fourteen, I became a khansama in training at the bungalow.

I found Murari helping chacha in the orchard at the back of the bungalow that had some mango and jamun trees and a kitchen garden where he had planted potatoes, peas and tomatoes. Murari was digging up the potatoes as I broke off some peas and began to munch on them.

'I'll tell the Kotwal Mem,' chacha said, busy putting newly plucked mangoes into a basket. 'A monkey called Bilal has eaten all the peas.'

'She counts them, doesn't she?'

'Of course she does! We malis are the biggest thieves in Amroli. We steal everything, even earth and grass.'

I settled in the shade of a mango tree. 'They all came to dinner last night—the paadri, Shore and Major Sahib. And they were talking about Gandhiji.'

Murari stopped digging and looked up at me. 'What were they saying about Bapu?'

I knew the mention of Gandhiji would get him interested. He went to a school run by the Arya Samaj and he knew a lot about our freedom fighters. He told me about Bapu's march to Dandi and had even gone to listen to Maulana Azad at a rally in Lucknow.

'Shore Mem was asking if the Congress is planning another protest, and our Sahib said that Bapu should go on another march because this time he would not survive it.' I took a deep breath, letting all my anger come to the surface. 'They would be happy if Bapu did not live. And they call Bapu all these nasty names.' Murari and chacha sat still, listening. 'And that Major Sahib! He wants the army to go and shoot the congresswallas if they go on another march.'

'Shoot them? Our azadi marchers are not armed,' chacha protested.

'Bapu is not going on a march,' Murari said. 'The Congress had a meeting in Bombay last week and they are starting a new protest called "Bharat Chhodo".'

'Leave India?'

Murari nodded. 'But there is a problem. The day after the rally, all the leaders were arrested and put in jail. Even Bapu.'

'Oh no! Then what will happen?'

‘As there are no leaders, it is the people who will have to run the protest. Now we have to lead the processions and rallies.’

‘We?’ chacha stared at his son. ‘What are you planning, Murari?’

‘Oh, nothing, Baba. I just meant we Indians,’ Murari said quickly. ‘I read in the papers that big protest marches are taking place everywhere in the cities. People are closing bazaars and offices and declaring hartals.’

‘What about the police?’

‘They have been beating up people with lathis and there has been some firing too.’ Then he looked at chacha’s anxious face and said, ‘Why are you looking so worried? I’m here in Amroli where nothing happens.’

Chacha bent over the mangoes again. ‘I can’t stop you and I know that this is a good cause, but if you do get into trouble, just make sure our Sahib does not find out. Or I’ll have no job.’

‘Ji baba, I promise.’

From then on, every afternoon when the adults were taking their naps, Murari and I would sneak out to the chai shop in the bazaar and get the latest news on the Bharat Chhodo andolan. We would listen to the latest gossip and get a chance to read the newspapers. The English papers were calling it the “Quit India” campaign. We heard of how Bapu and Kasturba were imprisoned at the Aga Khan palace near Pune while Pandit Nehru and Sardar Patel were in Ahmednagar Fort.

'The police always reserve the worst treatment for Panditji and Sardar Patel. They put them in solitary cells, do not give them medicines when they are ill, and give them bad food,' a man at the chai shop said. 'I think Panditji must have spent at least ten years in jail so far.'

As Murari explained, Bharat Chhodo was also a Bharat hartal. Everything was closed—schools, colleges, offices, law courts, bazaars, factories. Then people were coming out in processions singing patriotic songs, carrying our tricolour flag. Life had come to a stop all over India. The problems began when the police attacked the peaceful protesters with lathis or even fired at them. Then people became angry and the newspapers were full of reports of post offices, railway stations and police stations being set on fire.

'I thought we believed in satyagraha, non-violent protests?' I asked Murari. 'Isn't that what Bapu wanted?'

'Yes, he did, but as all the leaders are in jail, these protests are going out of control, and that is a mistake. My teacher at the Samaj School said that if we are violent, it gives the government an excuse to attack us. They are now calling out the army and will start shooting protesters. People don't understand that.'

'Can we win against their guns?' I asked, and Murari just shook his head.

At the bungalow the topic of conversation at the dining table changed. I think they had not expected the people to rise the way they had, even though the leaders were in prison. Government offices and law courts were shut because even government servants were refusing to work, and that was really worrying the Sahibs. It seemed that this had never happened before. I would report everything I heard at the dining table to Murari who would in turn tell his teachers and school friends.

It had begun to rain, and the humid weather made the Kotwal Mem sweat. Her temper got worse. None of us could get anything right. That morning, on a muggy, drizzly day, she marched into the kitchen and said, 'Gomes, last night the lamb curry was so hot, Sahib couldn't eat it. Too much chilly!'

Chef stared at her. 'How can that be, madam? I taste curry first, always. I cook for Sahib many, many years. I never put too much chilly.'

Kotwal Mem glared at him, her face going red. 'Are you saying that I'm lying?' The Mem was making a mistake, I thought. You never, ever said that the Chef cooked badly. Also, the kitchen boys and I had eaten some leftovers of the curry. It was delicious as always.

'Not lying, madam, but you very mistake. I always taste curry and I no put too much chilly.'

'Sahib was sweating ...' Kotwal Mem's voice was weakening at Chef's calm defiance. 'I saw it, Gomes.'

'It is rain time, madam, everyone sweat.' Then Chef stood straight, nearly reaching the height of the Mem, and declared, 'If I now bad cook madam then I go give up job!'

The whole kitchen was silent—the boy cleaning the pots, the masalchi grinding the spices, me stirring the pot

of dal, Abbu slicing the bread. Kotwal Mem swallowed. She knew it would be impossible to find another cook as good as Chef Gomes in Amroli. Also, she couldn't cook at all. We never saw her in the kitchen except occasionally to bake a cake.

'You don't have to quit, Gomes,' her voice was suddenly very soft and polite. 'Just be careful with the chilly.'

'I be always careful, madam,' Chef gave a disdainful nod and Kotwal Mem marched out.

Chef stood there, hands on his hips, watching her go. 'I think I go invite dat man Gandhi for dinner soon. He sure like my cooking.'

Abbu laughed. 'He's vegetarian.'

'No problem! I cook special spinach and potato bake for him. He like chilly?'

'I don't think so.'

'Then we invite that Sarojini Naidu. That lady look like she enjoy good food.' He waved a disdainful hand towards the door. 'Not like *her*, she got legs that look like dried bean sprouts, that one.'

So that was how that morning the whole staff at the bungalow joined the Quit India movement.

***

Then something happened. It was a rainy night. Ammi, Abbu and I had just finished dinner when there was a knock on the door.

'It's raining. Who's come now?' Ammi asked anxiously as Abbu opened the door. Shivpal chacha, soaked to the skin, came in.

'What's happened?' Abbu stared at him. 'Is anyone ill?'

'Murari's disappeared.' We stared at him in shock. 'I can't find him anywhere. He must have gone to join the protest.' Then he looked at me. 'Bilal, do you know anything? Did he say anything to you? Where could he go?'

I shook my head. 'He said nothing to me, chacha, but he has friends at the Arya Samaj school. Maybe they would know.'

'I went there. The principal told me that some teachers and boys have gone to Lucknow planning to join the march and he was pretty sure Murari has gone with them.' Chacha sat down and held his head. 'Why has he gone there? What will I do if he joins the protests?'

Abbu frowned. 'He's been to Lucknow before. Where does he stay?'

'There is a Samaj school and hostel there.'

'Let's go there and look for him.'

'We? What do we tell that woman? I can't tell her my son has gone to join a Satyagraha! She'll never give us leave.'

'She will. Leave it to me.' Abbu gave an odd, crooked smile. 'I'll need to go to Lucknow tomorrow to buy whiskey for the Sahib.'

'But Abbu, we are not out of whiskey. I just filled the whiskey decanter yesterday!' I said, puzzled.

‘I know,’ he said mysteriously. ‘Shivpal, be ready to leave by the ten o’clock bus. Once you have put the flowers in the drawing room, that woman will not look for you till the evening, and we’ll be back by afternoon.’

I stared at Abbu. ‘Memsahib checks the bar every week and counts the bottles. She’ll know we’re not out of whiskey. The decanter is full and there is half a bottle still left, more than enough for at least a week.’

He gave me a hard angry glare. ‘I don’t plan to steal the whiskey, if that’s what you’re thinking.’

‘Ji, of course not.’ But I wasn’t feeling so sure. As Ammi kept saying, one of these days his drinking would make him lose his job.

***

Next morning it was barely light when I began loitering around the bungalow. I had no work there but hung around the front garden where chacha was trimming the hedge. I carried in the flowers and left them in the drawing room for the Kotwal Mem to arrange later in cut glass vases. She and Sahib were having their morning tea in the verandah and I could hear the clink of china tea cups and the occasional gasp and grunt from Sahib.

I am always amazed at how much the angrez ate at every meal. First there were biscuits and cake at morning tea and then a breakfast of cutlets, eggs, bread and kedgeree. Lunch would be at least four courses with pulao, rotis, chicken or mutton curry, vegetables, dessert and cheese. Last night’s dinner had mulligatawny soup, roast chicken, lamb curry and rice, mutton pie, lamb dopyaza, rice pudding, walnut cake, cheese and bread …

CRAAASH! I raised my head and stood frozen to the spot. What was that? And then I heard Abbu shout, "Hai Allah!"

I ran towards the dining room with the Sahib and Mem thundering behind me. We came to a stop at the dining room door and what I saw made my heart sink to my shoes. There, next to the bar, Abbu stood, looking stunned. At his feet was the smashed crystal whiskey decanter and the yellow whiskey was growing into a pool on the floor before him.

'WHAT HAVE YOU DONE, ABDUL?' Sahib yelled.

'I'm sorry, Sahib …' Abbu's eyes were wide with fear. 'I was dusting the cupboard and it slipped from my hand … Sahib, please forgive me … this has never happened before … I'm so sorry …

Kotwal Mem widened her eyes. 'Ohhh, look! He's broken your whiskey decanter, Reggie!' She turned a furious gaze at Abbu. 'You will pay for this, Abdul!'

'Ji Memsahib.'

'I'm going to get Sahib to cut the cost of the decanter from your salary.'

'Ji Memsahib.'

Now it was time for me to speak. 'Oh Abbu, I filled the decanter only yesterday! There is very little of Sahib's whiskey left in the bottle.'

'And people are coming to dinner tomorrow!' Kotwal Men screamed.

That caught Sahib's attention and he ordered Abbu, 'Go to Lucknow by the morning bus! Get the whiskey today, Abdul. Jaldi! Jaldi!'

'And you'll pay for the whiskey too,' Kotwal Mem was by now whipping up her fury. 'Do you think I don't know about your drinking, Abdul? You must have stolen the whiskey and then broken the decanter to hide it.'

Abbu stood staring at her, stunned into silence by her words. Even Sahib seemed embarrassed and said, 'Oh Evie, quiet! You can see all the whiskey on the floor. That's enough!'

Abbu and I bent down and began to collect the broken pieces of glass on a newspaper as I heard the Sahib and Mem leave. I hid a smile. Abbu had planned the crash very carefully. There is a carpet under the dining table and the thick crystal decanter would not have broken if it had fallen on it. However, there was a patch of bare mosaic floor next to the bar and the broken glass lay there.

'Very clever, Abbu,' I said in Hindustani.

'Did you hear that woman?' he muttered under his breath. 'I have been with Sahib for twenty years and have never broken anything, not even a wine glass, and I have to pay for this old, cracked decanter? And when has she ever caught me stealing anything?'

'Will it all cost a lot?'

'I'll ask Sahib to cut some money every month. He'll agree. He's not a bad man—it's just that he doesn't speak up before that woman.'

Carrying away the broken glass, I thought, he's doing all this for Shivpal chacha. Usually he's so careful about money and loyal to Sahib. Smash Sahib's decanter and get fined for it? I had never thought Abbu would do something like this.

They were back by the afternoon bus and I was waiting anxiously by the gate as the tonga clopped up. Abbu, Shivpal chacha and a glum-looking Murari came down. They had found Murari at the hostel and chacha had reminded him of the promise he had made not to join the protests. So he had to come back, but clearly it made him very unhappy. Chacha, who was usually such a cheerful person, was looking very grim as he dragged Murari to his quarters. Murari must have planned to stay for a while at Lucknow because he was carrying a new cloth bag slung over a shoulder.

As Abbu and I carried in the cartons of whiskey and claret to the bar, the Kotwal Mem stood there, watching us. Then she said with her mean little smile, 'If this happens again, Abdul, you are out of a job.'

Abbu did not reply.

"Out of a job". That was one of her favourite phrases. It was so easy to say it. She did not understand what would happen if any of the servants lost their jobs. If the Sahib did not give a recommendation letter then no one would employ them, and their families would starve.

Sometimes I thought she forgot that we, the stupid brown natives, were human too. Just like her.

That afternoon I went looking for Murari. He sat outside their rooms and whispered, 'Meet me in the orchard. I've got something to show you.'

We met under a mango tree and he was carrying that cloth bag. 'I got it from Lucknow.' And he took out a rectangle of cloth in three colours with an odd image printed in the middle. 'Look!'

'What's that?'

'It's our flag!' There was a glitter of happiness in his eyes. 'Imagine, our very own flag, Bilal!'

The only flag I had seen was the angrez Union Jack that flew over the kutcheri building in town, and it was white, red and blue.

'Whose flag? This is saffron, white and green.'

'*Our flag,* you idiot! India's flag, the flag of the Congress party. I got it in Lucknow and I was going to carry it in the march today.'

I stared at the three strips of colour—a golden saffron, like the rising sun, on top; a gleaming white, like milk, in the middle, and then a stripe of deep green, the colour of new leaves … Oh, it was so beautiful! I pointed to the image in the middle. 'That looks like a charkha.'

'It is. Bapu says we should all spin thread on the charkha to help our weavers who have been deprived of work by the government because they want to sell us the factory cloth from Manchester.' He gave me the flag. 'Feel the cloth … it's khadi, you know, made by Indian weavers … the best in the world.'

He pointed to his kurta-pyjama. 'Baba and I have been wearing khadi for years, haven't you noticed?'

'From now on I'll wear it too.' I stroked the thick cloth. 'Imagine! Our very own flag of Hindustan!'

'One day we'll be free and then it will fly everywhere. On top of buildings, on flag poles. We'll carry them in processions ...'

'I'll make a kite in these three colours and fly it in the sky.'

We stood and laughed, our minds soaring with dreams. One day ...

'Does chacha know you have this?'

Murari shook his head. 'Don't tell anyone. The police can arrest you if you have this flag.'

'Arrest you? Hai Allah! Hide it carefully.'

A week later the Quit India movement arrived in Amroli. A hartal was announced by the Congress and the bazaar promptly shut down. Then as the protest marches began, Murari vanished again.

Shivpal chacha, Chef, Abbu and I sat waiting anxiously.

'He'll get hit by lathis and they'll arrest him,' chacha worried. 'I heard they are flogging the prisoners in prison.'

'Indian policemen torture Indian freedom fighters?' I asked, startled.

'The Indians are worse than the angrez.'

'I wish I had Murari's courage,' Abbu said, making chacha and me look at him in surprise. 'I have spent my life serving the angrez and I've been faithful to my salt, but they do not think of me as a human being. It's time we were free. This is our country. Let them go away and leave us to our fate.'

Chacha shook his head mournfully. 'Go on dreaming, Abdul. You and I will die as slaves, my friend.'

Murari came back late that night. He was dusty, tired and hungry, but his eyes were shining with excitement. Chef hurried into the kitchen and got food, and we heard of the march, of the police attacking them with lathis and riding their horses over people. But there was such a big crowd that they had to retreat into the police station and then the people took control of the town.

'Then we went and flew our flag over the kutcheri building! And we sang Bande Mataram!' Murari had come back with his flag on a bamboo pole. He laughed, his teeth gleaming in his dusty face. 'I carried the flag, Baba! I never let it fall from my hand!'

'Good. Now we'd better hide it,' Abbu said. He took the flag off the pole, folded it and said, 'I'll keep it for now. Take it from me when you join another march. It should not be found in these rooms. I heard the sahib tell that woman that the police are going from house to house searching for young men they suspect are freedom fighters. And you are from the Samaj School.' He turned to me. 'Bilal, put the pole in the garden shed.'

'The police won't come here! This is angrez cantonment, brother!' Chef looked shocked. 'Sahib is chief magistrate, no? He big, big officer Abdul.'

***

Chef Gomes was wrong. The police arrived the next evening. They had got a report that a young man carrying a flag had run into our lane and so they were searching all the houses. A police inspector and four constables marched in through the driveway and Sahib went to speak to them.

Kotwal Mem stood watching from the verandah and I saw a flash of fear in her eyes. What was she afraid of? We were the brown, stupid barbarians and they were the great white civilised people who were going to save us. They had the army, the police ... what could one boy with a flag do?

'Bilal, come here!' I heard Abbu call from the porch. 'I need help in the dining room.' I wanted to watch the police search, but had to go in. It was time to set the table for dinner.

As I was taking out the plates, ayah Dulari came in. 'Oh Abdul! They are opening everything and throwing the things about. Our rooms are a mess! They even made Chef Sahib open the rice and flour bins, and the spice box had to be emptied. He's very angry, and shouting at them. I have to tell Memsahib that dinner will be late. She won't like that!' Luckily ayah was asleep last night and did not know about the flag, otherwise she would have confessed the moment she saw the police.

'Have they found anything?'

'Of course not!'

We heard steps and turned to see the police inspector standing at the door staring at us. He was Indian with a fierce moustache curving on his cheeks but he was quite short and sort of stocky. He gave a suspicious glance and then asked Abbu, 'Who are you? What are you talking about?'

'I'm the khansama, Abdul Latif, Sahib, this is my son Bilal and that is ayah Dulari.'

Ayah stood frozen in panic and then did a deep namaskar. 'Namaste Inspector Sahib. We were talking about the search.'

My heart began to thud as the inspector strutted in and then walked slowly across the room, opening cupboards and peering into shelves. He then came to a stop in front of me. 'So, Bilal, you go into town yesterday?'

'No Sahib.' I cleared my throat nervously. 'I was here helping my father.' I was praying my face would not give me away.

'Where's the flag then?'

My heart was thudding so hard I could barely breathe. 'What flag, Sahib?' I tried to look puzzled, frowning hard.

'You haven't seen a three-coloured Congress flag?'

I shook my head. I'm not very good at lying and was afraid if I spoke, my voice would shake. Abbu, who was standing behind the inspector, now stepped forward and opened the cutlery drawer.

'Get back to work, Bilal. We have to finish setting the table, or dinner will be late.' With a silent sigh of relief I went back to the crockery ... the big plate, the soup plate, the wine glass ... as the inspector stood there watching us in silence.

Just then Kotwal Mem hurried in and stopped when she saw the inspector. 'What are you doing here, inspector?' she gave her usual fierce glare. 'This is my house. You won't find criminals here.'

The inspector seemed to wilt and shrink before our eyes and gave a sheepish smile. 'Just looking, madam.' He saluted and left the room.

'What cheek, coming in here!'

Ayah spoke. 'They search kitchen, Memsahib, and all things on the floor. So Gomes say dinner be late.'

'Oh bother! Tell the bawarchi to make just two courses ...' and she and ayah left the room.

Abbu and I gave huge sighs of relief. I stroked the tablecloth on the dining table and whispered in Hindustani, 'It stays here, Abbu?'

He nodded and whispered back. 'We'll take it away at night when they have gone to bed.'

Our flag lay snug under the snow white damask tablecloth, over which we had laid the table for dinner—plates, glasses, bowls and cutlery.

There was a hint of laughter in Abbu's voice. 'Let them have dinner over the saffron, white and green tonight. Get a real taste of Hindustan.'

Late that night we slid the flag out from under the table cloth, folded it and gave it to Murari who smuggled it out of the house. It vanished among the Congress workers of Amroli. Soon there were more marches and hartals, arrests and lathi charge in Amroli. Then the post office went up in flames and the police were so busy, they forgot about a running boy and his flag.

I have decided to become a cook, and Abbu likes the idea. Also Shivpal chacha has convinced him to send me to school again. So I go to school in the morning and train with Chef in the evenings and holidays. The Kotwal Mem has been so busy with gossip about the protests that she has not bothered us much. When Abbu got his salary, Sahib had forgotten to deduct any money for the broken decanter, and Abbu, of course, did not remind him. Let's see if the Mem remembers some day.

***

One evening Chef was teaching me the masala for chicken hot pot and chatting with Abbu who was sitting there smoking his hookah. Abbu said, 'When you grow up, Bilal, you'll cook in a restaurant owned by Indians.'

'I'll open one in Goa and he can come and be my chhota chef.'

'Watch my word, Chef, their days are numbered now. The angrez are going back, thank Allah.'

'How can you be so sure, man?'

'I know. I made a vow that day when the police came searching for the flag. They were looking for young boys and both Bilal and Murari would have been arrested if they had found the flag.'

I looked up from stirring the onions. 'What vow?'

'I've given up drinking,' and he smiled at my startled face. I hadn't realised there had been no binges in the past few weeks.

'I heard Sahib talking. They want to go back and he's thinking of taking early retirement.' Abbu shrugged. 'That woman's been begging him to do so and he knows it's all over.' Then he began to laugh. 'She thinks the Congress wallas will come here and burn down the bungalow.'

'Our Kotwal Mem got scared, eh?' Chef laughed. 'The big, white, sukht burra mem scared of us blackie Indians, heh heh …'

'Our time will come. Just wait and see ...'

'You wrong, man, these angrez—they want a thousand-year empire. They never leave India. They make too much money, man.'

'Five years. I'll give them five years and then they are all going home.' Abbu gave a small smile. 'Trust me, Chef. In five years we'll be free and I'll fly our very own tricolour flag from the top of this bungalow.'

I didn't believe him then but my Abbu was right.

....

HISTORICAL NOTE:

The first flag created by an Indian was shown by the freedom fighter Bhikaiji Cama in 1907 at a socialist conference in Germany. It was very different from the flag we have now. It had a green, a yellow and a bright red stripe. On the yellow band were the words "Bande Mataram" and on the red there was a half moon and a sun.

Then Mahatma Gandhi decided that the Congress Party needed a flag and the design that was chosen was by Pingali Venkayya, a farmer from Machilipatnam in Tamil Nadu. This flag was adopted in 1931 and it had the three stripes of saffron, white and green. On the white band in the middle there was the drawing of a charkha. This flag came to be called the Swaraj flag and it became the proud symbol of India's struggle for freedom. It was this flag that was carried by marchers during the Quit India campaign in 1942.

The flag of independent India has one change from the Swaraj flag. The charkha was replaced by the Ashoka chakra. It was adopted in 1947 by the Constituent Assembly that was writing the Indian Constitution. The chakra has twenty four spokes and it is dark blue. Dr S Radhakrishnan, who would later become the President of India, explained the significance of the three colours. Saffron stands for sacrifice, white is the light to the path of truth and green is our connection to our land. The flag is always made of hand-spun khadi cotton cloth.

....

MEETING GG GRANDPA

He is an old friend and we call him GG Grandpa or GG for short. You'll agree that "great-great-grandfather" is a real mouthful and his full name Jyotindra Mohan Chattopadhyay is even longer and is a total tongue-twister. We have read his name on the cover of many books because in his time old GG was famous as the author of the first English to Bengali and Bengali to English dictionary and then went on to write grammar books and alphabet primers and such boring stuff, and made pots and pots of money.

GG Grandpa is mentioned in literature encyclopaedias.

He was what my Dad calls an "intellectual giant", and I, a major headache.

Sometimes when I'm feeling friendly, I call him Droopy because he has the most amazing moustache I have ever seen—all bushy and drooping luxuriously over his upper lip. Of course I can't have a moustache like that because I'm a girl, but my twin Durjoy plans to grow one just like GG Grandpa.

'Durba, do they have moustache combs?' he once brooded, critically studying GG's photograph. 'Because you have to comb it, right? And maybe I'll have to oil it too.'

'I've heard coconut oil makes hair grow faster.'

'Nah! I can't have it growing too fast.'

'Still, some years to go, though; we are only eleven.'

GG's sepia photograph hangs above the mantelpiece in the drawing room of our house in North Kolkata. It shows him sitting on a high-backed, carved wooden chair and wearing dhoti and kurta. He has a shawl flung across one shoulder. Next to him there is a marble table where there is a pile of books he had written, including the famous dictionaries. We still have the marble table. It is in our grandma's room and his books are collecting dust in a bookcase. Nobody reads them, like ever!

This room is our favourite place in the house. I sit huddled in the squashy old sofa with the faded velvet cushions, reading murder mysteries, and Durjoy often sprawls on the moth-eaten carpet, doing his homework. Every time we look up, there's old GG the Droopy, staring down at us with a disapproving scowl, and it feels like he listens to all our conversations.

So we tell him jokes about chickens crossing the road or all the knock-knock stuff, and laugh like mad. I am convinced that writing grammar books kills your sense of humour because GG just stares back looking grim.

Once upon a time our family was really rich, which is why we have these carved ebony sofas, four-poster beds and pendulum clocks. GG used to travel around the city in a horse carriage and ordered books from London. Now the carpet is full of holes, the clocks stopped working years ago and we take a bus to school. I wonder what GG would think of my Grandma keeping her homeopathy medicine bottles on his antique marble side table.

That Saturday morning it was raining, so we were stuck at home, and Ma promptly ordered us to clear the cobwebs and dust the drawing room. I noticed that GG's picture was looking very dusty, and stood on a chair to clean the glass. So there he was, looking at me from six inches away.

'Hey! Good morning dear GG!' I thought I should greet him, just to be polite. 'How are the ulcers acting today?'

Behind me I heard Durjoy laugh. 'What makes you think he has ulcers?'

'Because he did not smile even while he was being photographed.' I bent to dust the mantelpiece. 'It's ulcers or indigestion.'

'You mean gas.'

Then I heard a small disapproving cough above me and a deep voice said, 'You two have no manners … I'm truly shocked!'

I froze.

'Durba,' Durjoy had dropped the broom and stood staring at me. 'Did you say something just now in a funny voice?'

I was dumbstruck. Right before me, GG was sitting up, turning his head and staring at me. Then, in the blink of an eye, he was still again.

'He moved!' I yelled. 'He spoke and then moved!'

'Who?' Durjoy was standing beside me.

'GG Grandpa! He said it was shocking, and he was staring at me. I am sure his eyeballs were moving!'

Durjoy jumped up on the chair beside me and leant forward to peer at GG. 'You're dreaming.'

'With my eyes open? While doing the dusting? You crazy? And you heard him too, speaking in that funny voice.'

Durjoy had to admit he had heard him. 'Oh Durba! Was that his ghost coming to haunt us?' he asked in a slightly shaky voice.

We stared in panic at the picture, but GG did not move again. So, feeling sort of puzzled and kind of nervous, we went back to our cobweb busting. Then the sky outside became very dark and it began to rain. The room became dim and gloomy and a bit scary, and both of us jumped when there was a sudden crack of thunder.

Now, whenever Durjoy is nervous, he tells a joke. He began, 'Hey, I heard a new one in school yesterday. A secretary goes into her boss's office and says, "There's a man outside with a moustache, waiting to see you." The boss replies, "Tell him I already have one".'

I began to laugh and then realised someone else was laughing with us. We turned and stared at the picture and there was GG grinning at us, showing a row of white teeth, his eyes all crinkling up. 'Good one about the moustache!' he guffawed. 'I have one too.'

'Oh boy!' I whispered. 'You're *really alive*!'

GG stopped laughing and looked down thoughtfully at us. 'Ah well, not exactly alive ... that would be difficult after being dead for umm ... what year is it?'

'Twenty twelve.'

'Oh my lord, we are in the twenty first century, are we? Then I've been dead for ninety seven years ... I'm *sort of alive,* shall we say?' he said with his eyes gleaming with amusement.

I realised that my mouth had fallen open and quickly closed it. GG leaned forward with a friendly smile and then took out a pair of spectacles from his kurta pocket. He perched them on his nose. These specs were interesting. They had no earpieces; instead, they were balanced on the bridge of his nose by a clip. A black ribbon hung at one end.

'Ah!' said GG in his deep, mellow voice. 'Let me look at you ... Durba and Durjoy, isn't it?'

My heart stopped thumping. Anyone who looked at us so kindly couldn't be dangerous, could he? I mean, who has ever heard of a ghost wearing glasses and laughing at moustache jokes?

'We are very pleased to meet you, sir,' I replied politely.

'Tell me something,' GG now sat with his legs crossed, his chin resting on his hand and his eyes bright with interest. 'Why do you have to call me GG? I mean my name is Jyotindra Mohan. It doesn't even have the alphabet "G" in it.'

'Actually it's short for great-great-grandfather,' Durjoy explained apologetically. 'It's very … er … long and …'

'Quite!' GG was nodding in a very understanding way. 'I would have done the same.' He raised a long, bony forefinger. 'As a matter of fact, all my friends called me JM.' The eyes crinkled again with a smile. 'Then you two are my Double Ds, my GG grandchildren?'

'You're nice,' I said. 'I thought you'd be all strict and stern.'

'Strict? What made you think that?' GG looked puzzled. 'Does the family history say that I was a stern person? Or that I had ulcers?'

'No, but you wrote dictionaries.'

'Hah! That was sheer pleasure.' Then he noticed we were looking confused. 'Dictionaries are full of such exciting, intriguing, beautiful words that are full of such wonderful images! Just think of words like delectable, majestic, aroma, musical, serene, serendipity, logical and fabulous.' He had a dreamy look in his eyes. 'Think of the meaning hidden in words like romantic, delicate, exquisite, picturesque, perfumed …'

I smiled. 'Yeah! They start off pictures in your head, don't they? A snow-covered mountain is majestic, a butterfly is delicate …'

'When I think of delectable ...' Durjoy added happily, 'I think of pulao and fish fry and mango chutney.'

'And the puja room is perfumed when Grandma lights the incense sticks.'

'Exactly!' GG clapped his hands in delight.' Now will you say dictionaries are boring?' We shook our heads. Once he explained it, somehow a dictionary became a fascinating book, with new discoveries in every page.

We pulled up two chairs and settled down for a chat. With the rushing sound of rain outside, the mood was just right for a conversation with a smiling ghost.

'Sometimes it gets so boring in this picture frame,' GG began. 'That is why I like the chicken jokes ...' he gave his toothy grin. 'I've been dying to laugh out loud for ages but I thought Durjoy would get scared.'

'What do you mean?' Durjoy sat up indignantly. 'You think Durba won't?'

'Girls are tough. Take my dear wife, your GG Grandma Mrinalini Debi. Once a burglar entered our village house in Tribeni and she chased him off with a chopping knife. She was just fourteen then!'

'She was married at *fourteen*?' I asked, quite shocked.

'Of course! She was twelve and I was sixteen when we were married.'

'She also wrote dictionaries like you?'

'Of course not!' GG looked shocked. 'She could barely read. She just cooked, ran the house and brought up the children. Enough work for a woman.'

'Hah! My Ma does all that *and* teaches in a college,' I said disdainfully. 'You wrote these famous books and GG Grandma never read any of them? That's truly sad, GG!' I gave a gusty sigh. 'Thank God this is the 21st century because I'm going to write murder mysteries one day.'

'Told you,' GG wriggled his eyebrows at Durjoy. 'Girls like all the blood and thunder things.' Then he sat up. 'You know I've been inside this frame for ages. I'd like a trip outside. Will you show me my home again?'

'Sure,' Durjoy said, 'but then you'll have to take us into the past to your time too. Can you do that?'

'I'd like to inform you, my dear GG Grandson,' he said loftily, 'that I'm an expert in time travelling!'

'Cooool!'

'Now watch ...' said GG Grandpa.

As we watched in amazement, a grey-white shimmering, ectoplasm-like thing came slipping out of the picture and then came floating and dancing behind us as we took a stroll around the house. As we were leaving the drawing room, I glanced back at the picture. There was just an empty frame hanging on the wall. The photograph of GG Grandpa had vanished!

I think only kids and animals can see ghosts because the maid, my mother and the gardener ignored us as we went past. But our cat Bindi, who was stretched out on my bed, took one look, gave a yowl, her tail went up straight in the air in panic and she went streaking off to hide under the bed.

'Heh heh ...' The ectoplasm laughed softly behind us. 'Looks like the GG cat does not like me.'

'You're sort of liquid ...' I tried to explain. 'Cats don't like water.'

'Ah! Of course!'

It was a really weird and freaky experience, taking your one hundred and seventy two year old great great grandpa around the house. It was tough explaining a television but he knew all about the radio and sort of understood what the iPod was all about. Then Durjoy showed him our computer. 'You could have written your dictionary on this,' he said, tapping away, writing all the words that GG had mentioned earlier—majestic and perfumed and picturesque. 'And see? The spellings get corrected automatically!'

'This is magic! True legerdemain!' said GG in worshipful tones, using a word I did not know the meaning of. I would have to check my dictionary. 'What a remarkable, revolutionary, futuristic invention!' went on GG, the living dictionary.

Once we were back in the drawing room, Durjoy said, 'Okay, GG, your turn now. You have to take us time-travelling, Boss.'

GG said, 'Of course! Close your eyes and hold your breath as I say the magic time-travelling mantra.' Then I heard him sing,

The British sing God Save the King
As Gandhiji goes marching.
Oh what a wonderful, magical mix
We are going to nineteen thirty six!

There was a whooshing sound in my ears. Then, 'Open your eyes!' GG called out. 'Welcome to Chowringhee!'

I looked around in astonishment. We were standing on a pavement on Chowringhee and a procession was coming down the road. All the people wore white khadi clothes and were carrying the tricolour flag. And most amazingly, GG was no longer a shimmering ectoplasm; he was all human.

'You're solid,' I grinned up at him and experimentally poked him in the arm. He was quite tall, broad-shouldered and looked impressive.

'I was alive in 1926, that's why. I saw all this happen.'

'What's happening, GG?'

'The freedom struggle is on! This is a Satyagraha march by the Congress Party and it is being led by Subhas Chandra Bose!'

'Oh maaan!'

The procession came closer and the noise got louder. We could see Netaji Subhas Chandra Bose in the distance leading the procession. Then suddenly our way was blocked by policemen riding horses and carrying long sticks.

'Time to go back,' GG said hurriedly. 'I don't want you two in the middle of a lathi charge. It'll happen in minutes. Quick! Hold your hands and close your eyes.' As I held my breath, I heard him say,

Computers and cricket and TV
In Kolkata there is so much to see.
So let's open time's revolving door
Its twenty twelve once more!

With a whoosh and a crash we were back in our drawing room. Opening my eyes, I looked at the picture and blinked in shock. GG Grandpa was back in the frame, all still, silent and solemn.

'That was awesome, GG Grandpa! Thank you so much!'

Did we see GG Grandpa wink at us or did we imagine it?

....

HISTORICAL NOTE

GG the Droopy is a combination of two men. The first is my own great grandfather Kshetra Mohan Sen Gupta who did write dictionaries, though I doubt he made much money. We have a fading sepia photograph where you can see his magnificent droopy moustache! Also, he did not smile. This story is also in the memory of his son, my grandfather Nirmal Chandra Sen Gupta, who was a poet and a freedom fighter and a follower of Mahatma Gandhi.

....

COMING SOON

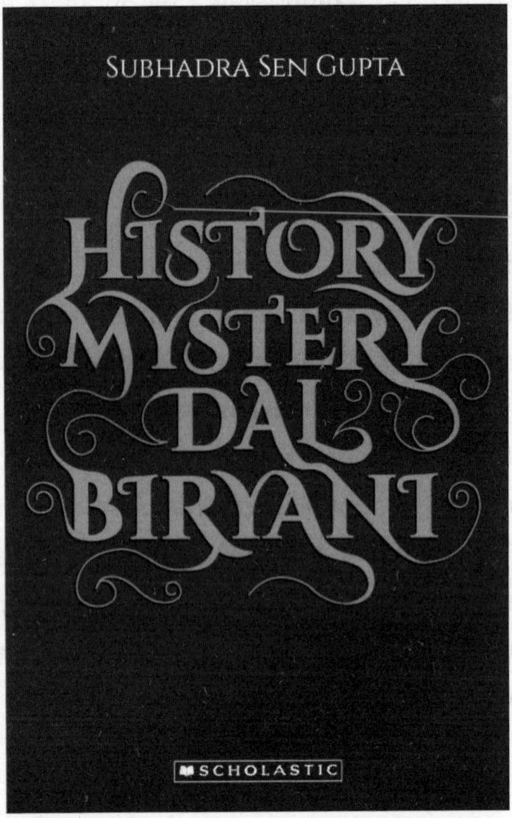
SUBHADRA SEN GUPTA
HISTORY
MYSTERY
DAL
BIRYANI
SCHOLASTIC